Who Is This Man?
The Jonathan Chronicles

Robert Picou

RIVER BIRCH PRESS

Daphne, Alabama

River Birch Press
P.O. Box 868, Daphne, AL 36526

I want to dedicate this book to my wife

who stood by me and encouraged me through the

long and sometimes tedious process of writing

and to my daughters and their families.

I am particularly grateful to my friends

for their continuous excitement in seeing

the next chapter as I was writing.

Contents

Characters (in order of appearance):

Jonathan: main character, from a wealthy family, trained as a scribe and a lawyer

Ruben: man who attacks Jonathan

Mathias: AKA Nikephoros, "victory maker," Greek slave and caretaker of Jonathan

Miriam: woman who tends Jonathan's wound, Ruben's wife

Tabitha: Ruben and Miriam's daughter

Martha of Simon Boethus: Jonathan's mother

Joshua bar Gamaliel: Jonathan's father

Shaphrah: meaning "beautiful," Jonathan's older sister

Lucius Atticus: Roman centurion, friend of Joshua bar Gamaliel

Cornelius Rufus Salvius: commander of the Roman legions

Nicodemus: AKA Bunai Ben Gurion, very wealthy, High Council member

Abigail: meaning "joy," Jonathan's younger sister

Quintus Magnus: Roman Tribune, Governor of Caesarea

Gaius Claudius: secretary to Quintus Magnus

Amir Ben Remiel of the House of Gosh: member of Herod's court

Hanel: Amir Ben Remiel's son

Stephen: Jonathan's friend, disciple of Jesus of Nazerath

Gamaliel bar Yaakov: Jonathan's grandfather, land owner, farmer, lives in Hebron

Introduction

I believe that I was led to write this story. For a long time, I thought about how to begin and what to say after I started. I knew the beginning of the story. It was about a young Jewish man who was the son of a member of the ruling class on his way to see the crucifixion. Jesus had healed him, and he wanted to help. How, he knew not, but along the way he was attacked by a man whose brother was being crucified alongside Jesus. He was attacked because he was the son of a member of the Sanhedrin.

The story that follows is about this young man and the struggles he faces as he begins to find out the truth about his father and the Sanhedrin, falls in love with his attacker's beautiful daughter, and tries to determine who was the man some called Messiah.

Research shows that the religious ruling class felt contempt for the average individual living in Jerusalem. They were Pharisees and Sadducees, self-centered and puffed up with pride, who considered themselves righteous, unlike the dirty masses. They used their power to gain riches even at the expense of their countrymen. In other words, they had an outward form of godliness but were corrupt, unfeeling, and greedy on the inside.

This is the world that Jesus came into. He did miracle after miracle to show who he was and preached a message of repentance, but the people of his day were not interested in repentance, much like our world today. What the people wanted was a Messiah to deliver them from the Romans. That's what their scriptures promised, or so they thought. What they saw was a man filled with love and compassion for the ordinary person. He was a lowly man, who treated the poor, the sinful, the despised, and the prostitute with kindness as he preached repentance to them.

I sat at my computer and marveled at how the words and the story unfolded before me. Most of the time, I did not know where I was going with the story or what was going to happen next. All I knew was that I wanted to share how the death of Jesus of Nazareth impacted the people of his day.

Let's consider what happened to people after Jesus rose from the dead. How did the righteous rulers of the Sanhedrin deal with the continuing "rebellion" of this Jewish carpenter? What happened to Caiaphas—to Pontius Pilate? What happened to Nicodemus?

I imagined the disappointment in the minds and hearts of those who followed him and believed that he was the Messiah. They remember declaring him as the king as he entered Jerusalem on the tenth of Nissan when they cried, "Hosannah to the Son of David. Blessed is the King who comes in the name of the Lord!" Then he was gone, or so they thought.

Who was this man that brought such love to the world? Was he truly the Messiah that they were waiting for?

1

THE CRUCIFIXION OF JESUS

The door closed behind me. I looked around at the courtyard, the plants, the flowers, and the trees. It was a peaceful place I'd enjoyed for many years. I saw things that reminded me of my past—special places that were built for me to enjoy, such as the flowers and waterfalls that had brought peace to my shattered body. I knew I should go back in the house and apologize. I was not used to arguing with my mother, but she didn't know the Teacher, and now the Romans have him. *Why? What could he have done to deserve this?* I didn't hesitate. I knew what I had to do.

As I left the courtyard, I wondered if I could do anything. I had no power over the Romans. I knew that I could not affect the release of a Roman prisoner, especially one condemned to death. All I knew was that I had to go. I had to try.

The streets were mostly deserted. A few servants were out sweeping, but the market was not yet open. As I came to an intersection, I heard the rumble of a chariot. I stepped back and froze. As I did, two white horses came running wildly past me. They were pulling a wooden chariot with two men in it. I recognized one as a centurion. The other was driving. They were gone almost as fast as they appeared. I leaned against the building. Trembling.

My mind began to relive an incident when I was five years old. I was crossing a street with my father and older sister. The street was much like the one I was now on—maybe a little wider or perhaps a little narrower. I couldn't remember, but I did remember that someone called my name, and I turned to look back. Suddenly I was under the hooves of a horse, and then I was hit by the chariot. The Roman driver didn't even stop. I remembered wondering about my sister before I lost consciousness.

When I awoke, I was at home, lying in my bed, but I could not feel my legs. I was told I would never walk again. I would now be a prisoner of my bed. My life would change forever. My dream of one day entering the Holy Place to burn incense in the tabernacle or even to offer the Show Bread would never be fulfilled because I was lame. But the Teacher changed all that, and now I must help him if I can. So I headed for the praetorium.

The streets were unfamiliar, so I stopped to ask directions from a woman who was setting up her stand for the market. Suddenly a man came from around the stall. He was tall, thin, and dirty. He began yelling at me, grabbed my robe, shook me, and threw me to the ground. He put his foot on my chest, pointed his finger in my face, and said, "It's your fault! You and your kind! Holy men! You are nothing but robbers and thieves! You should die, not him!"

He picked me up again and slapped me several times, and I fell back to the ground. I felt him kick me. Again. Harder this time. As I opened my eyes, he was grabbing a rock. He stood over me, the rock held high. I could not watch. I closed my eyes and waited, knowing the blow was coming. But it didn't come.

When I opened my eyes again, I saw Mathias, his great arms holding the man. There was no rock now in his hands. There were no longer flames in his eyes. The man crumbled to the ground and began to cry.

Then I heard him say, "I'm sorry. Forgive me. Please forgive me."

Mathias helped me to my feet and stood between the attacker and me. I was glad that Mathias had shown up when he did. He was a slave in my father's house and had cared for me since the accident that left me lame. He was Greek, very tall, and strong enough to handle my broken body since I was five years old. He had also become a good friend.

"Your mother sent me to follow you," he told me.

"I'm glad you did! Do you have any idea why he attacked me? What have I done to him?"

"With your permission, I will find out."

I nodded. In one smooth motion, Mathias plucked the man from the ground and stood him erect. I noticed his feet were off the ground, and the man was gasping for breath.

"Mathias, put him down. He won't hurt me." Mathias put him down, but he was having a hard time standing.

"Why did you attack me? What is my fault and what did I steal from you?" I asked and waited. Finally, the man spoke, but there was fear in his voice.

"My brother dies today. He will be crucified for being a thief, but he had no choice. He borrowed money from a member of the Sanhedrin, and when it came due, he could not pay so they took his farm. Without his farm he could not earn money to pay his taxes or feed his family, so he stole. He was caught and now he must die."

"So, why attack me? I'm not a member of the Sanhedrin."

"Your father is! It was he who lent my brother the money!"

For an instant, his eyes flashed, and I saw the hatred again.

"What is your name, and why do you lie? My father would never do something like that!"

But the man remained silent. As I looked around, I saw the distrust and anger on the faces of those standing around watching. Was that look for me or him?

Suddenly I could hear the murmuring. People began to move back to their stands. Faces looked down at the ground. The Romans were coming. Mathias moved me off the street and into an alcove of a local home. About twelve soldiers marched quickly past us. They were heading somewhere and not interested in what was happening on the street. Mathias told me that they were the death squad—the men who did the crucifixions.

"Mathias, I must have a plain cloak. The one I am wearing is too noticeable. Get me something else, quickly."

"But how, master?"

"I don't know. Buy one. Steal one. I don't care. Just get something to cover what I'm wearing. Please."

Mathias walked away as I watched a few individuals from the crowd gather around my attacker, cover him with a dark cloak, and help him disappear down the alley. Like a shadow at midday, he was gone. I knew I would get no answers from him. Why would he lie about my father?

A woman from the market crossed the road toward me. She was tall and thin. Her outer garment was wool, intricately woven and freshly washed. She carried a small cup of water and a towel.

"Your head is bleeding," she said as she reached for my head to see the cut. She turned me so that she could get a better look.

I suddenly realized that my head was hurting and reached up to feel the wound. Gently, she moved my hand away and began to wipe away the blood.

"It's not too bad, but it will need some oil and a bandage." She said as she motioned to someone across the street.

She turned to me and said, "My name is Miriam. The man who attacked you is my husband. I am deeply sorry. He is not a violent man. Please forgive him! He is terribly upset about his brother."

"What is his name?" I commanded. She continued to dress my wound. Suddenly I noticed that there was someone with us, a young girl. She was about my age or maybe younger. She was shorter than I was, thin with an olive complexion. Her hair was long, black, and straight, and there was a glow about her. She was beautiful, as beautiful as my sister Shaphrah. She moved with such grace and beauty; I could not keep my eyes off her.

"This is my daughter Tabitha. She's brought some oil and a bandage for your wound."

I tried to say something, but I was afraid to speak. Afraid that if I spoke, she would somehow disappear. I nodded and tried to smile.

Then she spoke to me, "Please forgive my father. I have never seen him like that before. He is such a kind man, always helping others. Please don't have him arrested." Her words were soft and gentle. Her face was radiant, and her eyes begging. I could not disappoint her.

"Please," I said. "Say no more about it. It is forgotten. I

would like to know why he lied about my father, though."

"He didn't," said Miriam. "Your father lent his brother money and took a mortgage on his farm. When the debt was not paid in full on the due date, your father confiscated the farm and removed the family to the streets. They stayed with us for a while, then went to live with his father. When the taxes were due, the Romans took his daughter because he could not pay. She was younger than Tabitha, just thirteen."

Just then, Mathias arrived, and I remembered where I was going before I was attacked. He had an old cloak made of gray wool and a dark-colored sash. I stepped into a courtyard to change. I removed my blue prayer shawl with four phylacteries containing my favorite scriptures and handed it to Mathias. I put on the old gray cloak and closed it with the sash. Wearing these clothes along with the bandage on my head, I hoped I would not be recognized.

As we were leaving, an old woman came up to Miriam and said, "They are going to crucify him. We thought he was the Messiah, but they are going to kill him!"

⟢◆⟣

The streets were becoming crowded. People were gathering to see the procession of the condemned. Some were there to see the criminal Barabbas crucified, but they heard that he was set free and that Jesus was to take his place. I moved closer to the crowd in the praetorium. I could see most of the Sanhedrin gathered with their fists held high and yelling, "Crucify him, crucify him!" The crowd joined in, "Away with him. Crucify him."

Pilate stood. The noise and the yelling stopped. Pilate called for water to wash his hands. "I am innocent of the blood of this just person. You see to it." Then I heard my father's voice as he spoke, "His blood be on us and on our children."

The soldiers took Jesus away as the crowd dispersed. I hid behind people who were standing, waiting. I didn't want to be recognized. I looked around; Mathias was nowhere to be seen. The sun was blazing hot, but more people were gathering. The crowd pushed me forward, which made it hard to stand. I tried to move to the back of the throng but could not get through. Guards were leading the procession with spears to clear the way.

The first man to be crucified passed by us. He was just skin and bones, but the stripes on his back had mostly healed. He had to be prodded along with the point of a spear. Members of the Sanhedrin were walking behind. They looked like conquering soldiers leading their captives.

As Jesus passed, he fell. His face hit the cobblestone. The beam fell against his head. I noticed the crown of thorns cutting deeper into his skin. The centurion grabbed the man in front of me and ordered him to carry the cross. I looked into Jesus' eyes, but there was no fear, only determination and sorrow. His face was disfigured, and his right eye had almost totally swollen shut. Parts of his beard were missing.

Jesus struggled to get up. His hands and knees were bleeding from the fall, but he marched forward at a slow pace. Then I noticed my father, along with Caiaphas and some members of the Sanhedrin walking behind Jesus. I was afraid that I would be recognized. My heart was pounding as they slowly moved on with the procession. After the third man came by, the crowd began to follow. I joined in behind two men who were talking.

"He deserves what he gets. He's a blasphemer!" The other man said, "He made us believe that he was the Messiah. Now they are going to kill him. When will God deliver us from the Romans?"

Others were lamenting about how he was a good man and didn't deserve to die. I heard a man behind me say, "He should never have exposed the chief priest and his puppets. They are as crooked as the Romans. He wasn't guilty of anything. Why do you think they arrested and tried him in the middle of the night?"

I was glad for the clothing that hid my identity. I did not want to be identified with the High Council. Finally, the streets began to narrow, and many people returned home.

A small group around the High Priest still taunted Jesus. "Son of God you say! Where is your father now? We will watch. Maybe he will come and save you!"

They all laughed. Some spit on him. One even tried to kick him but almost fell to the ground. I smiled. It would have served him right to fall on his face. Once we arrived at the crucifixion site, Caiaphas called a soldier and pointed at Jesus.

"This one first," he said. "And make sure that he can see the temple as he dies!" He barked those orders loud enough for everyone to hear. Then he quietly spoke with some of the men in his group.

After that, Caiaphas and the other members of the Sanhedrin, including my father, left to return to the temple. It was Passover. They had work to do.

The soldiers had their work to do also. The four soldiers assigned to Jesus began by pushing him to the ground on top of the cross he had just carried. They stretched him out on the cross with his arms being pulled so hard I thought they were going to come out of their sockets. I could see the pain on Jesus' face.

Then two soldiers put their weight on his right arm as one of the soldiers grabbed a mallet and some nails out of a big leather bag. As he approached Jesus, I closed my eyes, but I could still hear him scream with pain as the mallet struck the nail. I could hear the cries and screams of the other victims who were being crucified too. *What cruelty,* I thought. *How could someone do this? Why?* Surely Jesus did not deserve this. No one did!

I opened my eyes to watch as his cross was raised and dropped into place. I looked away. The sun still blazed. The sky was blue, but clouds were gathering. I turned back to look at him. Flies were everywhere. One of the soldiers was using a whip to chase the dogs off. "Wait! It's not your turn yet," he said as the dogs tried to get past him. Some of the other soldiers were playing dice. The prisoners would die slowly, and these soldiers were not in a hurry to leave.

Then I heard Jesus say, "Father, forgive them for they know not what they do." *How could he say that? How could he forgive these men who did this to him?*

The sky began to darken. Time passed. It kept getting darker, and people were frightened. Most of the onlookers left as they tried finding their way home. I felt a hand on my shoulder and looked around. It was Mathias.

"We should go, Master. Your family will be worried about you."

"No. I want to see this through to the end."

There was one man and some women standing close to the cross of Jesus. I wondered who they were and why the centurion seemed to protect them and favor them from the other onlookers. *Did they know him? Were they his followers?*

The darkness closed in on us, and the wind picked up. I was having a hard time standing. As I looked up to the cross, I heard Jesus say, "It is finished." His head rolled forward. His body became limp. I knew he was dead.

Suddenly the earth began to shake so violently that I couldn't stand. I fell to my knees and looked at Jesus. It was so dark; I could barely see him. The earthquake lasted only for a few minutes. When it was over, everything returned to normal. The sun was shining, and the wind was still. There were tears in my eyes. At the cross, the women were crying. The man led one of the women away. She was older. Maybe she was his mother. She could barely walk.

Mathias helped me up. "We must get home before the Seder starts. I'll be in trouble with your father if you are late."

"Let me worry about my father," I said. "But I don't want you getting in trouble for me." So, we turned to leave. It seemed forever before we got home. Even though most of the streets were empty, I traveled very slowly. I couldn't get over what I had seen and learned. I really didn't want to go home. Mathias reminded me to remove the old cloak and sash he had given me earlier.

2

A JEWISH PASSOVER

When we arrived home, I stopped in the courtyard, but Mathias went into the house. I tried to reclaim the peace that I once knew in this place. The garden was beautiful. The red everlastings in the center fountain were surrounded by blue lupines. In the far corner next to another fountain was a host of purple mandrakes. I moved to my favorite fountain, its water flowing over a hill of rocks into a fishpond. The scene was soothing, but I had no peace. My mind was troubled by what I had seen and heard today. I still could not believe that my father was involved in the death of such an innocent man. The door opened, and my mother came out of the house. She sat down beside me.

"Are you okay, Jonathan?" She noticed the cut on my forehead and touched it gently. "How did this happen?"

"It's a long story and we don't have time," I replied.

"Will you tell me later?" she asked.

"Yes. Right now, I have to speak to my father!"

"No! Do not discuss what happened today with your father. Not tonight. He has had an exceedingly difficult day and is in no mood to talk about anything."

"I'll bet that his day was not as difficult as those crucified today!"

"Jonathan, these are difficult times. Your father and the

rulers of the council are trying to keep the peace so that Rome does not destroy our laws, our customs, or our nation. Please try to understand. Now, tell me, will your friend Stephen be sharing Passover with us as he has in the past?"

"I haven't talked to him today, but after what father just did, I doubt if Stephen or any of my friends will be sharing Passover with us."

"Jonathan, it is not for you to question the actions of your father. You are his son and as such must support him no matter what he does. He has a very precarious position in the Sanhedrin. He must always appear to support Annas and Caiaphas. It is your father's desire to become chief priest one day. Think of what that would mean to this family and to you."

"Mother, his lineage will not allow him to become high priest."

"No, my son. His lineage won't, but my lineage will. I am of the Boethus line. Your father could be appointed chief priest just like Caiaphas was, through his wife."

"I'm not interested in that anymore. The Sanhedrin is corrupt. How could they condemn a great prophet of God? Jesus was good and just. We all knew he came from God because of his miracles, but they were jealous of him and had him killed. Mother, he healed me! He took my hands and I stood up! I have been walking ever since."

"Son, you must put this aside for tonight. There will be another time to talk with your father about such things. Not tonight. We cannot spoil this great feast with such talk or the anger that it will bring. Please, if you love me, do not speak of this again today."

I considered what she said. "As you wish, Mother."

She went into the house. It was getting dark. I pulled my prayer shawl over my head and repeated a favorite prayer, "Not to us, O Lord, not to us but to your name be the glory, because of your love and faithfulness," then slipped quietly into the house.

My father's brother, Elam, had arrived with his family. They were going to celebrate the Seder with us. Mother began to hurry us along, sending us upstairs. I started toward the stairs but was interrupted by a young servant girl. She had a towel, a bowl of water, and a clean pair of sandals. She knelt and removed the sandals from my feet. Then she began to wash my feet. I sat down and looked at her. She has been a part of our house for almost a year, and I didn't even know her name. I didn't realize how much I was like my father. Mother called again, and I ran up the stairs.

The room was beautiful. The great oak table with brass legs was set for the Passover feast. Two ebony palm trees were inlaid into the top of the table. Cups of wine were set by each place along with several silver dipping bowls containing salted vinegar for the bitter herbs and charoseth for the matzah. The bitter herbs were there to remind us of the bitterness of slavery, and the charoseth reminded us of the hard labor of making bricks. Shabbat candles, vegetables, unleavened bread, and roasted lamb were all in their proper place.

"Jonathan, your place is here, next to me." my father said. I was shocked. My place had changed from the lowest spot around the table to the one of "honored guest." Now that I have use of my legs, I am his son.

Mother lit the Shabbat candles, and my father said the prayer of sanctification: "*Barukh atah Adoni Eloheinu melekh ha'olam asher kid'shanu b'mitzvotav v'tzivanu l'hadlik nersel shabbat.*" For my family, the Passover had begun. We dipped bitter herbs and drank warm wine. We prayed and sang psalms. My uncle's son asked the required questions I used to ask:

> Why is this night different from all other nights? On all other nights we eat leavened or unleavened bread, but this night only unleavened bread. On all other nights we eat all kinds of herbs, but this night only bitter herbs. Why do we dip the herbs twice? On all other nights we eat meat roasted, stewed, or boiled, but on this night why only roasted meat?

As my father answered his questions by telling the history of our people, our enslavement in Egypt, our deliverance from Pharaoh, and our wilderness experience, I began to see the significance of this day. The first born of Israel were saved by the sacrifice of a lamb. Sons and daughters of Egypt died, but the sons and daughters of Israel were not under the same judgment as long as they were covered by blood—the blood of a sacrificed lamb. I saw the striped matzah on the table. It reminded me of the striped body of Jesus. I remember going with my father to the sellers to get a lamb for this Seder and presenting it to the priests in the temple for approval. That was the same day that Jesus made his entrance into Jerusalem with the approval of the people. It was the tenth day of Nisan as described in the Torah.

Suddenly we were singing psalms again. We ate bitter herbs dipped in the salted vinegar. We completed the ritual hand washing, ate the sacrificed lamb, broke matzah, dipped it in the charoseth, and sang more psalms. After the fourth cup of wine, everyone recited the post-meal blessing.

The Passover meal was over, and the servants were clearing the table. Guests were rising and walking around. My mother was looking at me. I could see the fear in her eyes that I would not honor her request and discuss things with my father that she had asked me not to discuss. I looked at her and smiled.

My father placed his hand on my shoulder and said, "Jonathan, we will be going on a business trip at the beginning of the week. There is a little trouble in Magdala, and I want to make sure that none of our people are involved in it."

"Why am I going?" I replied.

"Son, it is time you begin to take the responsibility that is yours. I have trained you to be a scribe and a lawyer, so you know the law and can scribe official documents, which may have to be completed while we are there."

"I don't understand. Why would that be necessary?"

"You will see" was all he said. Then he got up and began talking with his brother as they both left the room. I wanted to follow, but my mother called me to her.

"Thank you, Jonathan. I appreciate you not talking to your father tonight. Maybe you can speak with him on the way to Magdala."

"Did you know about that, Mother?"

"You know your father tells me nothing."

"That's not an answer. But it really doesn't matter. I must go with him."

3

They Will Come for Me

"It's time to get up, my husband. I know that we don't have work today, but we must pray. The Lord requires it of us," Miriam said as she touched Ruben softly.

He stirred, waking up to a small plate of dates and matzah. He looked at his wife. She was smiling, but he couldn't. Last night they participated in his family's Passover meal. There was sadness throughout since his brother had been crucified. There was no feasting, no rejoicing, no deliverance.

"We have been following Jesus for almost a year," he said. "We heard him teach and saw the power of his hands. We didn't expect this. Even after his arrest, I thought, we all thought, that He would somehow break free and deliver himself and the others from death. That He would call down from heaven the wrath of God on the Romans and the corrupt Sanhedrin and that all of Israel would be delivered from the oppression that makes our lives almost unbearable. Instead, the Teacher died, just like my brother. The hope he gave us is gone. Adoni has deserted us. Why pray?" he said softly. "Tomorrow or the next day the temple guards will show up here to arrest me for hurting that young man. I don't know what came over me, but I'm sure that I will pay for it."

"Father, you're wrong. I don't think that he will have you

arrested," said Tabitha as she entered the room. "He promised that it was all forgotten."

"I don't believe it. What do we know of this young man?" said Ruben. "If he is like his father, he will bring the guards to the door to make sure they do it right!"

Miriam bent over and kissed her husband. "I know a lot about 'this young man' as you call him. His name is Jonathan, and he is the son of Joshua bar Gamaliel. He was involved in an accident when he was five years old and could not use his legs. The big man who kept you from killing him is his slave, given to him by a Roman after the accident. I was told that Jonathan was healed by Jesus when he was with his father in Magdala about three months ago and I too don't believe he will have you arrested."

"You can believe what you want, but once he tells his father, the decision will be made for him," said Ruben as he got out of bed. "I know that I can't go today because of the Sabbath, but on the first day of the week I might go to Emmaus and disappear for a while."

"Alone?" asked Miriam.

"No, not alone. I'll take a friend."

"Who?"

"Cleopas. I think that he has relatives in Emmaus. He's also a follower of Jesus and sometimes he stays with the disciples. Don't worry, I'll only be gone a day or two, unless they come for me." He got dressed and went outside.

"I wonder where he is and what he's doing right now," said Tabitha.

"Your father is in the barn, feeding the animals," replied Miriam.

"Mother, I'm not talking about Father."

"Jonathan?"

"Yes, mother. He was a very handsome young man. I don't think that he is like his father." Tabitha smiled. She opened her arms and spun around.

"Stop!" her mother said. "This house is in mourning because of your uncle. You would do well not to think on Jonathan again, and do not speak of him to your father, ever. Do you understand?"

"Yes, Mother." She heard the words come out of her mouth, but she knew that she didn't mean them.

"I want you to make sure that all of the cheese is properly wrapped and ready for the market at the beginning of the week and clean the cheese cloths that were used yesterday. Do you understand?" Miriam asked. "No more foolishness."

"But it's the Sabbath," Tabitha complained. "We are not supposed to work on the Sabbath, Mother."

"Your father will not be with us when the market opens again, so we must complete this work today. God will understand."

4

MY SISTER SHAPHRAH

It was the next afternoon. Stephen stopped by to say he was sorry for not letting me know that he was not coming to Passover with us. He was with some friends who were upset about the death of Jesus, and he thought it best to stay with them and help. I understood. That was Stephen's way, always thinking of others.

When he left, I returned to the desk in my room, which also acted as my library. I knew that someone had entered; I could smell the perfume. I thought it was my mother coming to find out how I got the cut on my head, but, to my surprise, it was my sister Shaphrah. Her name meant "beautiful" and fit her perfectly. Her smile lit up my room. She came to where I was sitting and hugged me.

"It's so good to see you," I said. "Have you come for a visit?"

"I've come to see you and to see how you are doing. How do you like walking again? Also to find out how you got that nasty cut on your head."

"So, Mother sent you," I said. She smiled. "You know, you're really very beautiful when you smile."

"That's not an answer," she said. "Are you going to tell me, or do I have to get the information from Mathias?"

"You probably already have, and you want to check my

story against his!" I smiled as I said it. Then we both laughed out loud.

"I'm sure that it happened as Mathias said. He's very honest."

She looked at me and said, "He said something about a girl. A young girl. He said that you really had trouble talking after you noticed her. Was she very pretty?"

"Almost as pretty as you," I said.

"Almost," she said. "So, I'm still the most beautiful. Are you going to see her again?"

"I don't think Father or Mother would want me to see her again."

"Is that going to stop you?" she asked.

"No. I don't think it will. My heart says that I will visit her again. Soon, I hope," I answered.

"That's good," she said. "Sometimes I believe that God orchestrates things in our lives that happen for our good. This may be one of those times. But, please don't tell Mother or Father that I said this. They think that I'm a proper Hebrew wife."

"Aren't you?" I asked.

"Of course," she laughed.

"Really?"

The smile left her face but not her eyes. "Ever since I heard the Teacher, Jesus, I've been wondering. Wondering if this ritualistic religion we practice is really what Adoni wants. Wondering if all those rules made by our religious leaders brings us closer to Adoni or if those rules just help fill their treasuries."

"Remember, he was crucified for his teachings by the very people who make those rules," I told her.

"I know. That's what scares me, Jonathan. I was hoping that you had some insight. After all, you talked to him when he healed you, didn't you?"

"Not really. He took my hands and told me to stand. When I stood up, I looked down at my legs. They were straight and sturdy. When I looked up again, he was gone. He did say that the accident that left me lame was not because of sin but for the glory of God. I don't know how he knew that I was lame because of an accident, or that I had been wondering if the accident happened because of my sin or my father's sin, but he knew my thoughts."

"Who was this man?" she asked. "Really, who was he?"

"I don't know," I responded, "but I will find out."

"When you find out, would you please let me know." It wasn't a question; it was a request.

We spent the remainder of the afternoon talking about our childhood, remembering fondly the games we played and the times we cried together. Finally, Mother called us for the evening meal, and Shaphrah took my arm as we walked together. I noticed that she nodded at Mother, and it seemed that the subject of my head was settled.

Again, Father mentioned that we would leave early in the morning to go to Magdala. He had business to conduct there and reminded me to pack my legal scrolls and some parchment. The meal was festive with my oldest sister and her new son there. Mother occupied her with questions about her husband, were there plans for more children, did she need help with the household planning, and giving her advice about child rearing. I noticed that my younger sister, Abigail, was not happy, and I tried to talk to her during the meal. After the meal was over, I decided to follow Abigail to find out what was going on with her, but before I could find her, I was called back to be with the family.

Father explained that we would take the shortest route through Samaria because we were traveling with Commander Lucius Atticus and a centuria of Roman soldiers. Lucius was a centurion and a friend of my father, but the Romans didn't care about our hatred of the Samaritans. Since we would not be traveling on major roadways, he expected to stop in Sychar the first night and Tiberias the second night, which means we would be in Magdala early the following morning.

5

THE TRIP TO MAGDALA

Mathias woke me. "We must go, master. Your father waits for us."

I got up and noticed that it was still dark. As I was dressing, Mathias told me that my clothes and scrolls were already packed and loaded. I heard my father giving orders to the servants, then he called for me. Mathias and I joined him as he entered the courtyard. He was in a hurry.

Outside the courtyard, I saw the Roman soldiers. It was a unit of about one hundred men with horses and full battle gear. The order was given for us to mount, and I was handed the reins of my horse and helped up by Mathias, who then swung onto his mount with great ease.

"You'll have to teach me how to do that one day," I told him. He just smiled.

Father was the last to be mounted. He was riding next to Lucius, who gave the command to move. As we proceeded through the streets of Jerusalem, the noise of the horse's hooves must have awakened many people. We passed the marketplace where I had seen Tabitha, but no one was there. I wished to see her again.

Soon we were out of the city gate and on our way to Magdala. The eastern horizon had a glimmer of light, and I knew that it would be about an hour before the sun was up and shining. I also knew that the day was going to be hot and dry.

Occasionally we were passed by travelers who were on their way to Jerusalem and knew that traveling in the coolness of the early morning was better than traveling during the heat of the day. But the Romans we were with would travel the whole day. They appeared unaffected by the heat or the speed at which we were traveling. By evening we were approaching Sychor. I didn't know about the others, but I needed the rest.

After the tents were pitched, I thought I would finally get a chance to talk to my father about the information I had gotten from Miriam, Tabitha's mother. Plus, I wanted to confront him about the crucifixion of Jesus. Mathias informed me that my father was with the Roman commander, Lucius, and would not be back until much later. I laid down on the cot prepared for me and closed my eyes for just a minute.

When I awoke, the sun was almost up, and everyone was getting ready to move again. Once again, there was no sign of my father. I dressed and joined the others just as the troops were mounting. The atmosphere seemed a little more stressed than yesterday. Mathias informed me that our mounts were in the rear of the column. Father would continue to ride with Lucius for a while longer but would be joining us by mid-morning. It seemed that the Romans didn't want to appear that they showed any favor to Jews. As we got to the rear of the column, Mathias placed a cloth around my neck.

"Put this over your face to reduce the amount of dust you will eat," he said. Then he mounted his horse.

"Remind me to thank God for my guardian angel," I said. Then I smiled, grabbed the rein of my horse, and swung into the saddle with great ease. Mathias looked at me and grinned.

"Very good!" he said. "You are getting stronger."

"Thanks to your training," I said.

The second day seemed longer than the first. Father didn't come to the rear until late afternoon. Mathias dropped back, and Father came alongside me.

"We will be staying in Tiberias tonight," he said. "They have many hot springs bath houses there. I can't wait to soak in one to get this travel dirt off and get into some fresh clothes."

"Father, I would like some of your time to discuss several things."

"What things, Jonathan?" he asked.

I wasn't quite ready to tell him, so I just said, "Things to do with finances."

He smiled, "Sure, we'll talk tonight." We heard a trumpet sound, and he rode toward the front of the column. We had arrived at the city of Tiberias.

The walled city had two great circular towers standing guard over the wooden entrance gate. A narrow bridge over a man-made moat forced the column to close as it crossed over to enter the city. Once in the city, there was a large, paved palisade that allowed the Roman soldiers to form ranks and put on a show of discipline and horsemanship. Leading from the palisade was the longest street I'd ever seen. It seemed to go on forever and had beautiful marble columns standing as sentinels on both sides of the avenue. The rest of the city was laid out in Roman fashion with straight streets covered in cobblestone. As we passed through the palisade, I could see the Theater of Tiberius nestled in the side of the mountain, sitting like a crown above the rest of the city. This was truly a Roman city sitting in the middle of Galilee.

We rode for some time before we arrived at the inn. When I dismounted, I could barely move. Everything was sore, from my neck to my feet. Father promised that I would get a good rubdown after spending time in a hot springs bath. I couldn't wait, hoping that I could be revived enough to complete the journey to Magdala the next day.

After my bath, Mathias brought me to my room and helped me unpack for the night and tomorrow's journey. Then he repacked my things and asked me if I needed anything. When I asked if he could bring me a particular scroll from my baggage, he said that my father ordered that no one was to touch those but me.

He indicated that the evening meal was being served and I should join my father in the main dining area. When I did, we were joined by Lucius and another Roman officer, Cornelius. It was then that I heard about the expected attack on Magdala by Jewish rebels. Lucius didn't know when the attack was going to happen but was on his way there to reinforce the small garrison stationed in Magdala. Father indicated that he needed to get to Magdala to complete some especially important business and asked for advice from Lucius.

I was shocked. I had never heard him ask for advice before. Before Lucius could say anything, a man from the inn came and informed my father that there was someone there to see him and that it was especially important. Father left the table, and I didn't see him again that night.

⮞◆⮜

The day started off golden. The sun was coming up in the east, and there was a coolness that promised the day would be fulfilling. Miriam kissed Ruben goodbye, although she thought his trip was unnecessary. As he left, he looked back to see if anyone was following him. No one was.

Miriam and Tabitha pushed the cheese cart to the market and began to set up their stall for the day's business. Most of the other shop owners were setting up too. The smell of fresh bread filled the air, and Miriam knew that this would draw customers to the market. Tabitha unwrapped the cheeses and placed the different types in their area for display. Soon, people would be coming. Servants would be buying cheese for their masters, and women would be selecting cheese for the day's meal.

A lot of talk was shared among the shop owners about what had happened at Passover when the Romans crucified Jesus. One of Miriam's friends asked where her husband was, thinking that he had been jailed for trying to kill one of the Pharisees' sons. Miriam explained that he had to go out of town and that nothing had happened about that incident. He would be back in a day or two. Others were talking about the crucifixion of Jesus. Someone expressed their sorrow over Ruben's brother and asked how his family was doing. Soon, customers began to arrive, and the marketplace became a hub of human activity. Tabitha hoped to see Jonathan at the marketplace again, but the day passed without her wish being fulfilled.

That evening at home, there was a soft knock at the door. It was late. Miriam hesitated to go to the door, but she heard the knock again.

"Who's there?" she asked.

"Ruben, your husband," came the response.

When she opened the door, Ruben hurried in, but his actions were strange. It was like he almost couldn't stand still or sit down.

"Are you alright?" she asked, looking him over.

"He's alive! I saw him!" His eyes glowed, and his face was full of excitement.

"Who...who's alive?" she asked.

"Jesus! The Teacher is alive. I saw him. Spoke with him."

"Ruben. You're mad. Jesus was crucified. He can't be alive."

He stood in front of her, grabbed her shoulders, looked in her eyes, and said, "I know he was crucified, but he is alive!"

She found it hard to believe, but she said to her husband, "Come sit down. Tell me about what you saw. Tell me. I want to know."

He couldn't sit down. He paced back and forth like a caged animal as he told her about the events of the day.

"I met Cleopas at the gate like we planned. He told me that some of the women in his company had seen Jesus' empty tomb early this morning and that they had spoken to an angel. We were discussing all these things as we walked when a stranger joined us and asked what we were talking about. Cleopas explained everything that had happened to Jesus during Passover and about what the women said they saw. Then the stranger began to explain the writings of Moses and the prophets to us. I could not believe my ears. I understood what he was saying. Suddenly it made perfect sense."

"What made sense, Ruben?"

"Scripture clearly predicted that the Messiah would have

to suffer all these things before he could come into his glory," he said. "He showed how scripture was fulfilled by what happened to Jesus. We listened. Our hearts were on fire, and we did not recognize the very man we were talking about. We asked him to stay and have a meal with us. As he broke bread at the meal and blessed it, our eyes were opened, and we realized that it was Jesus! Then he disappeared."

"What do you mean 'he disappeared'?" she asked.

"He vanished! Disappeared! One minute he was breaking bread, and the next minute he was gone. Like he had never been there!"

"What did you do?"

"We hurried back to Jerusalem. When we got to where the disciples were, we told them what had happened. Just about the time we were finished telling the story, Jesus stood in the room. No one let him in, but he was there. I'm telling you, he's alive!"

Miriam sat in disbelief. How could this be?

6

THE SKIRMISH AT MAGDALA

When Mathias woke me the next morning, I found out that we were preparing to go to Magdala within the hour. The servants, except for Mathias, would be staying in Tiberias until called for, but Father and I would be on our way with the scrolls to Magdala within the hour. Father told me that it was necessary for us to arrive in Magdala as soon as possible. Mathias attached my scrolls to his mount and asked me if I needed help getting on my horse. I grabbed the reins and swung into the saddle. Mathias just smiled. The seven-mile journey would take only an hour or so on horseback, but Father's timing was all wrong.

As we came over the rise of the road that led into the valley before Magdala, I was alarmed by what I saw. We had arrived just in time to see the battle between the Romans and about three hundred Jewish zealots. They had amassed before the city and challenged the small garrison stationed at Magdala. As we watched, about one hundred Roman soldiers formed in front of the city gates, facing their opponents. Lucius and his cavalry had taken up positions behind the zealots cutting off their escape. Mathias rode up beside me to get a better view of what was happening.

"Have you seen battles before, Mathias?" I asked.

"I fought the Romans many times in many battles. They

are exceedingly difficult to defeat. I was captured during the last battle that I fought against them. That's when I became a slave."

I looked at him, understanding a little better his lot in life.

"Why are they waiting?" I asked. Just then, a command was given, and the garrison soldiers formed a wedge with interlocking shields and began a slow march toward the zealots. At the same time, Lucius and his cavalry unit began to move forward, concentrating on the flanks of the rebels. Then, suddenly, I heard the sound of a ram's horn. It was a signal. The trapped rebels rushed to attack the advancing Romans in front of them as other zealots came running out from behind the rocks to attack the cavalry. It appeared there were another three to four hundred rebels designed to squeeze the Romans in a trap.

The cavalry spun around and attacked the closing force. The oncoming rebels used slings to hurl rocks at their enemy, but they were no match for mounted cavalry. Then, the gates of the city swung open, and out came two regiments of Roman legionaries. They separated, forming two groups that took positions on the flanks of the garrison troops. As one man, the back rows threw their pilas into the zealots, causing the deaths of many. It was obvious that the Romans were winning the battle, but the zealots would not give up. They knew that death or slavery would be the result.

Lucius and his cavalry were now making their way into the main body of the rebels. One of the zealots removed a pila from a fallen comrade and threw it at Lucius. It struck his horse, which tumbled to the ground. As I watched, I felt anger well up inside of me.

"Father, we have to help them!" I said.

"Lucius can take care of himself," he responded.

"I'm not talking about Lucius," I responded. "I'm talking about our countrymen. They are being slaughtered! Killed by the Romans."

"They made their decision," he said. "Remember that, Jonathan. For now, there is nothing we can do for those men. Jews must learn that there is no Messiah and no deliverance from the Romans."

While my father was speaking to me, I watched in horror as Lucius dispatched three zealots who attacked him, almost decapitating one of them. After that, fighting was going on around him, but no one challenged him. Then a large man who was leading the zealots came forward. Father said that his name was Levi bar Alpheus, a seller of wool, now a rebel leader. The conflict did not last long. Levi was quickly wounded, having his right thigh sliced open. He desperately tried to attack Lucius, but his wound made him slow. Lucius countered his blow and knocked Levi to the ground. Levi struggled to get up to a defensive position, but Lucius just waited, like a cat playing with a toy. There was another round of swordplay, and Levi wound up on the ground again, this time with a sword at his throat. The battle was over. Some of the rebels tried to escape, but the archers in the tower killed most of them. The rest of the zealots would be in chains by evening.

Cornelius Rufus Salvius, commander of the Roman legions, rode toward us. "You must return to Tiberias. No one goes into or out of Magdala today," he said.

Father began to object, but Cornelius just held up his hand. Father stopped talking.

"I know that you need to enter the city and that you claim that your reasons are important, but today, no one goes in or out of the city. Because of your friendship with Lucius, I will allow you to enter the city tomorrow."

He turned and rode away. Father was not happy, but we returned to Tiberias.

Later that evening Father summoned me to his quarters.

"Jonathan, you said that you wanted to talk to me?"

"Yes, I did," I replied.

"What's on your mind?" he asked.

"Well, first of all, what is so important about getting to Magdala?"

"Your sister is getting married. I know this comes as a shock to you, as it did to your mother, but I have decided to give her to a young man in Magdala."

"Does Abigail know this young man?

"That doesn't make any difference. We need to be connected to this family in Magdala. They are very influential. The father is a part of Herod's court, Amir Ben Remiel of the House of Gosh. His son, Hanel, is highly sought after. Your sister's mohar is to be some land next to our fish factory. I've tried to buy that land from Amir for several years. It's a valuable piece of land. You are here to write the Ketubah contract."

"Father, you're selling my sister to this man for a piece of land. Will this make her happy?"

"Yes. She is part of my family and will do what I say. Her happiness, her joy should come by being obedient to her father."

"Does she know?"

"She's met him. We were supposed to come to Magdala

the week before Passover, finish the contract, and announce the engagement, but I was unable to get away because of that rebel, Jesus."

"He was not a rebel." My voice was louder than it should have been. I reminded myself that it was my father that I was speaking to and tried to calm down.

"Oh, I know," Father said. He rose and walked toward me. "You think that he was the Messiah, a great holy man because he did a few miracles—the son of God—the deliverer of Israel. Well, the Romans are still here. They crucified him!"

"They didn't. You did!"

"I know you were there. I know all about it. I know about the man who attacked you because of his worthless brother who was being crucified too. His brother was a common criminal, like your Jesus. Then, you did nothing about it. You're weak, Jonathan. I also know that you stayed and watched Jesus die while I went to the temple to worship Adoni."

"And I heard the curse you brought down on me and all my offspring when you yelled that His blood be upon us and our offspring," I responded, trying to keep my composure as I spoke. "Why would you say something like that?"

"Annas and Caiaphas were pleased with it," he replied.

"I imagine they were," I said.

Father took two steps toward me and slapped my face hard. "Don't you ever speak disrespectfully of the high priest again."

I reached up and touched my mouth. There was a trickle of blood along my lower lip. I raised my head and looked at my father, and for the first time, I saw fear in his eyes.

"Don't you ever strike me again," I said to him. I turned and walked out of his room. The door slammed behind me. I returned to my room where Mathias had a cold wet towel for me. I looked at him.

"I heard," was all he said.

"Thank you, Mathias."

A short time later, there was a knock at the door. "Enter," I said. My father entered the room. He walked over to me and looked at my cheek.

"I'm sorry, Jonathan. I'm deeply sorry. I should never have slapped you. I was angry. Not with you, but with the situation I find myself in. I feel confident that by now the young man will be promised to some other person and that the opportunity will have passed."

I looked at him but said nothing.

"In addition, I found out that Jesus' disciples have stolen his body and claimed that he has risen from the dead. Like that could happen. Caiaphas wants me back in Jerusalem to help track down those deceivers, but we are so close to finalizing the marriage if it is still possible. What do you think I should do?"

"Why ask me. I'm weak, remember," I said coldly.

He turned and walked to the door. As he put his hand on the latch, he looked back at me and said, "I am your father. I forbid you to go to the tomb of Jesus. It is off limits to you. Understand? Further, I do not want you talking with Nicodemus or Joseph, his friend. I will not have you becoming a follower of this pretend Messiah. Believe me, their days are numbered." The door slammed behind him.

7

THE PROMISE OF HOPE

Miriam felt like she had wings. Since talking to Ruben, she knew in her heart that Jesus had risen from the grave. It was just a matter of time, she thought before he would return Israel to the Jews and rid the land of the Romans.

"That's a beautiful song," said Tabitha.

"What song?"

"The one you are singing, Mother. I've heard it sung in the temple, but it didn't sound as beautiful as the way you are singing it now."

"I didn't realize that I was singing out loud. You need to get your chores done. Don't forget to milk the goats. We are running short on goat cheese and need the milk to make more. Go on. We don't have much time. You are going with your father today to the market. It seems we sell more cheese when you are there. I guess it's your pretty face or your happy disposition that attracts customers. Hurry now."

Tabitha grabbed her apron as she went outside. Her chores were before her, but her mind was not on what she was doing. She thought that maybe today she would get a visit from Jonathan. Soon the milking would be done, and she would be on her way to the market to set up shop with her father. As soon as the milking was done, she brought the milk to her mother, who gently poured it into the warming pot.

"Tabitha, get the vinegar from the barn and bring it to me. You'll find a skin of it hanging on the back door. Hurry. Your father has already left with the cheese wagon. Hopefully I will have the curd ready to be washed by the time the both of you return this afternoon."

"Yes, Mother," she answered. She retrieved the skin of vinegar and brought it to her mother.

"Do you need my help now, Mother?"

"Not now. Go! Catch up to your father and help him get the stall set up."

Tabitha ran into the house, hung up her apron, and grabbed a head covering. She checked her clothing and ran off to find her father.

By the time she had caught up to him, he was almost at the marketplace. She helped him as he set up the wagon and displayed the cheeses. Two large wine skins were hanging on the wagon, and she asked her father what they were for.

"Those are two skins of posca. I must bring them to the Antonia fortress today. The Roman soldiers drink this vinegar and water mixture daily. I was lucky enough to be able to sell these two skins to them," he told her. "Maybe this will become a regular thing."

Zirea was filling her stall with freshly baked matzah bread. Tabitha knew that it wouldn't be long before customers arrived. Ruben began telling everyone about his experience from a few days before when he saw the risen Jesus. People could hardly believe his story. Some of them said they had heard the disciples of Jesus stole his body and declared that he had risen from the dead. Ruben explained that he was with the disciples when Jesus, himself, stood in the room, ate fish and honeycomb, and spoke with his followers. An old man pulled him aside and cautioned him.

"The temple guards are looking for his disciples or anyone who can tell them where the disciples are hiding. If you value your freedom, do not talk about such things at this market," he said.

Ruben smiled. "He's alive! He's alive! I've seen him. He spoke to me...to me!"

"That may be so," the old man said. "But if you continue saying that at this marketplace, you will be jailed."

Customers began to arrive. Soon the marketplace became very crowded. Tabitha was concerned that they would run out of goat cheese. She was thankful that her mother was making more today.

It was just after mid-day when her father asked her if she could manage the stall on her own.

"If I need help, Ziera will help me," she told him.

He took the two skins of posca and put them on his shoulders. Then he headed to the fortress of Antonia next to the temple. Looking back, he said, "I'll be right back." Ruben headed toward the Antonia tower, but he was slowed down due to the congestion. It seemed that everyone was out in the streets, making it difficult to make easy progress. After he left the upper city, he turned east toward the temple. He had never been to the fortress, so he didn't know what to expect. He finally made it to the Warren Gate and the second quarter. Traveling along the temple wall northward, he arrived at the steps leading up to the gate between the two front towers of the Antonia fortress.

This fortress was a slap in the face of all Jews. One of the four corner towers reached above the walls of the temple, allowing the Romans to keep watch of what went on in the temple. Even in the sacred temple, Jews were being watched by the Romans. The water skins were very heavy, and Ruben considered laying them down to catch his breath. However, once he noticed the two guards at the top of the stairs, he decided not to put them down.

At the top of the stairs, he was questioned by one of the guards and sent to the quartermaster within the walls. Passing through the gate, he entered a large open quarter where soldiers were attacking each other using practice swords. They were padded but used no shields. Ruben saw a soldier sitting at a small wooden table who motioned him to approach. As he went over to the table, one of the practicing soldiers walked toward him.

"What do you want?" asked the quartermaster.

"I've been instructed by Quintus Magnus to bring this posca," Ruben answered.

"Do you normally supply the garrison with posca?" asked the quartermaster.

"No sir, but Quintus Magnus said that you needed extra due to the heat, and he enjoyed the taste of my drink."

"Give me a cup," said Lucius Atticus, the soldier who walked over from the practice field. A cup was quickly brought to him. He poured a cupful and handed it to Ruben.

"Let's see if you enjoy your drink," said Lucius. He had a devilish grin on his face as though he had just caught a criminal.

"Sure," answered Ruben and drank the cup dry. "I needed that after carrying those skins from the marketplace."

Lucius laughed and told the quartermaster to pay for the posca. Ruben gladly accepted the Roman coins, turned, and walked toward the gate.

"Stop!" was the order he heard. His heart was pounding as he turned to see Lucius with a cup of posca held high.

"Quintus is right. Your drink is exceptionally good. Bring more as soon as you can."

Ruben bowed and left the fortress. He turned south and headed for the gate to the upper city. Two temple guards were following him. His pace quickened, but they caught up with him.

"Come with us. The high priest wants to talk with you," one of the guards told him.

"Why? I've done nothing," he responded, but the guards each grabbed an arm and escorted him into the temple complex until he came to one of the spacious rooms next to the temple. The guards ushered him into the room where Caiaphas was waiting.

"Ruben. It was good of you to come," Caiaphas said. "We need to talk."

"With respects, your honor, I really didn't have a choice."

"No, I suspect not," Caiaphas said as he looked over the guards who were almost a head taller than the man they were guarding. "We were told that you've been spreading rumors about the rebel Jesus. That he's somehow risen from the dead. That you even talked to him, saw him eat a meal, and watched him as he interacted with his disciples. Is this true?"

Ruben remembered the old man's advice and now wished he would have been careful about what he said. "Yes, it's true."

"You should know better than to spread false hope to poor people. We know that it was the disciples who stole his body and claimed that he had risen," Caiaphas said.

"But I saw him. I talked to him. He explained the scriptures to us so that we could understand why he was crucified and how all these things occurred to fulfill scripture and—"

"That's enough!!" Caiaphas yelled. "Do you presume to know more than I do? I am the high priest. I have memorized the Torah, the Nevi'im, and the Ketuvim. Don't you think that if this man could possibly be the Messiah that I would have recognized it and welcomed him as our king? He is an imposter; he's no more the Messiah than you or I, for that matter. Now, here you are spreading rumors about something you have no knowledge."

Turning to one of the priests, he said, "What should we do with someone who spreads false testimony?

"He should appear before the council tomorrow," came the answer.

"Hold him until tomorrow," ordered Caiaphas. "We will see if he remembers better in the morning."

8

Nicodemus Knows

I kept the hood over my head and close to my face. The rain had stopped, but I didn't want my father to learn where I was or with whom I was talking.

As I entered the gate, I noticed that the house was large and well maintained. Marbled tile radiated from the central fountain, which was extremely large, made of white granite containing gold flecks, and very unusual.

Water streamed from the brass palm tree that topped the granite structure and ran into several channels of moving water. The garden was beautiful with flowers in bloom everywhere. Trees and shrubs were well manicured. Several servants were sweeping, cleaning up after the rainstorm. Some were tending the fruit trees and the vegetables in the far corner of the garden.

An older man approached me. "How can I help you, master Jonathan?" he asked.

"I've come to see, Nicodemus. Is he in?" I wondered how the servant knew my name.

"Yes, he is expecting you," he replied. "I will take you to him."

We crossed the courtyard and entered the house through a massive Cyprus door with brass hinges. After a short hallway, I was ushered into a large room. It was about twice the size of my room at home. Light seemed to come from everywhere, yet I couldn't see any lamps or windows. The room was wrapped in cedar panels. Along the wall close to the ceiling were carvings of palm trees, lattice works in olivewood and ebony, and bronze pomegranates embedded in every other panel.

Nicodemus was at the other end, looking at a wall covered by shelves made of poplar that contained an almost countless number of scrolls. The oak desk between us was exceptionally large and had what appeared to be gold inlays of palm trees and pomegranates along the edges. He reached up and grabbed a particularly well-used scroll, then turned to look at me. His eyes seemed to smile as he saw me.

"So, young Jonathan, you've come to show me that Jesus healed you? But this I already know."

"How do you know?"

"Your father told me, several months ago. He was used to you not being able to walk. When you were healed, he didn't know what to do or how to handle it, so we talked. One day, shortly after it happened, we were talking about Jesus, and he said that he thought you were healed by Jesus at Simon's house in Magdala."

"He knew? He always told me he believed that I was healed because of the cleansing ritual in the water pool at Magdala."

"I know that the water at Magdala is the purest in all Israel, but even your father knows that you could not have been healed without supernatural intervention, and water is not supernatural."

"And Jesus is?"

He paused, then he said, "Jesus is who he says he is."

"You mean he was who he said he was? He's dead." My words came out forcefully.

Nicodemus smiled like he knew something I didn't know.

"Jonathan, have you been to the tomb where Jesus was buried?"

"No, my father has forbidden me to go there. He says that the followers of Jesus came and stole his body, then claimed that he rose from the dead, like that's possible."

"He knows better," said Nicodemus, "but I can see why he is telling you these things."

"Are you telling me that my father is lying to me? That Jesus was really raised from the dead?"

"I'm telling you what I know. Jesus is no longer in that grave, and that fact had nothing to do with his disciples. "

"How do you know this?"

"Have a seat, young man."

I sat in a beautiful leather chair with X-shaped bronzed legs and ornate armrests. Nicodemus opened the scroll before him and read. It was a reading from the Psalms.

No wonder my heart is glad and I rejoice. My body rests in safety for you will not leave my soul among the dead or allow your holy one to rot in the grave.

He took another scroll from the desk and opened it to a marked section:

Yet it was our weaknesses he carried; it was our sorrows that weighed him down and we thought his troubles were a punishment from God, a punishment for his own sins. But he was pierced for our rebellion crushed for our sins. He was beaten so we could be whole. He was whipped so we could be healed. All of us, like sheep, have strayed away. We have left God's paths to follow our own. Yet the Lord laid on him the sins of us all.

"Isaiah wrote those words about the Messiah," I said. "Are you telling me that Jesus was the Prophet; the one spoken of by Moses; the one we must hear and obey—the Moshiach?"

"Not he was," said Nicodemus. "He is! As I said, Jesus is no longer in that grave. He has been raised from the dead, Jonathan."

"You expect me to believe that?"

"Jonathan! You above all! You have memorized the Torah, you know the psalms, the prophets, and the writings about the coming Messiah. You can probably quote the passages written in Genesis, Numbers, Isaiah, Psalms, Jeremiah, and Zechariah, and all the other passages that speak of him. Israel has waited for him to come for over a thousand years, and he's here, now!"

"And so are the Romans," I said. "Besides, I'm not sure that I believe in a resurrection from the dead."

"If you would have talked to the soldiers who kept watch of the tomb and heard what they had to say, you would not doubt, young man."

"Did you talk to them?"

"Yes, but I am under a solemn oath not to repeat what was said. I can only tell you that a great deal of money has been spent to make the disciples of Jesus seem guilty of perpetrating a fraud. They did not steal his body from the tomb. He walked out."

I sat there. Silent. Thinking. Writings identifying the Messiah coursed through my mind. I thought of the Torah, the prophets, and the psalms. *Could this possibly be true?*

"But if it is true, why doesn't my father and the others in the Sanhedrin believe that Jesus is the Messiah?" I asked.

"Your father is afraid—afraid to disagree with the high priest. As for the others, you know that the Pharisees believe that they are the only ones who can anoint the Messiah. Since Jesus did not come to ask for their anointing but continued to break their man-made rules, they could not accept him as the Messiah, even if they thought that he might be. Add to that Jesus' act of overturning the money changers and setting loose the doves, you can see why Jesus was not popular with the Sanhedrin."

"But aren't these men servants of God?" I asked. I knew the answer to that question, but I wanted to hear someone else say it.

Nicodemus sat down in a large, high-backed chair. He stroked his long gray beard with both hands for a few minutes, then looked at me and said, "Would you tell me about your meeting with Jesus at Magdala?"

"What do you want to know?" I asked.

"Did he say anything to you? Were the others present when he healed you? How did he heal you—what did he do?"

I took a deep breath. It was a story that I would never tire of telling. "My father was invited to the house of Rabbi Simon's for the evening meal, and I was allowed to go with him. The main table was very crowded with important guests, so I was served in the courtyard of Simon's house. Jesus' disciples were there at one end of the garden. They were not being served. I could hear some of the conversation from the main table, but I did not understand very much.

"Suddenly, Jesus came out of the house. There was a

woman behind him. He stopped and looked at me. Then he said, 'Your accident was not because of sin, it was so the glory of God could be revealed.' Then he took my hands and told me to stand and walk. I felt something surge through me at that moment. I stood. Mathias went to grab me, but he stopped when Jesus held up his hand. Suddenly I could walk. I looked down at my legs; they were straight and supporting me. When I looked up, Jesus was gone, along with his disciples. A servant went to tell my father that I was standing and walking. When he came out, he looked at me with such disbelief that I thought that I was dreaming."

"What did he say?" asked Nicodemus

"My father? He said something about a ritual cleansing in a sacred pool. I don't know. At that moment I was experiencing something that I had not experienced since I was five years old. I was walking, although I was upset with myself because I had said nothing to Jesus. I hadn't even thanked him. I wanted to run after him and embrace him as thanks for what he had done.

Simon and his guests were all congratulating my father and celebrating with him. No one thought to ask me what happened. When my father came to embrace me, I told him that Jesus had healed me. He said to be quiet, and we would talk about it later. I obeyed him, but I shouldn't have. I should have shouted the truth about my healing from the highest roof top. I failed him, and I failed him again when he was crucified."

Nicodemus looked at me then said, "Did you know that I had a private meeting with Jesus? It was about a year ago at Passover."

"What did he say to you?" I asked.

"He said that if I was not born again, I could not see the kingdom of God." he answered.

"I don't understand! Born again?"

He looked at me. "At first I didn't understand either. Jesus continued by saying that which is born of flesh is flesh, and that which is born of the Spirit is spirit. Then I understood what he was saying."

"I still don't understand," I answered.

"Jonathan, what do we say when a baby is born? It is a new life. The child's life has begun. That is flesh born of flesh. New life. What Jesus was talking about was a spiritual birth, or rebirth —a new spiritual life."

"So, that caused you to believe in him and become one of his followers?"

"No," Nicodemus replied. "Not at that time. I believed he was a great prophet. A man sent from God to teach us and help us in our journey. It wasn't until I saw the tomb where he was laid and heard the testimony of the guards that I believed. Now I understand that he was talking about becoming a new person—death to life—life to new life.

I am a Jew by birth and now a follower of Jesus. I made that choice. I'm still a Jew. But I know that the man who died on that cross was God's Son. The promised One. The anointed One. His blood now takes the place of the blood of lambs, rams, bulls, or goats that we sacrifice in the temple constantly."

I thought, *is Jesus the Anointed One who was to be killed appearing to have accomplished nothing as spoken of in the writings of Daniel? Could he possibly be the suffering Messiah in the writings of Zechariah?* We've been looking for the deliverer, someone who would deliver us from the Romans and not from our sins. Maybe my father was right. God will not deliver the Jews from the Romans.

As I got up to leave, Nicodemus had one more thing to say. "Jonathan, when Jesus died, the veil was torn."

"What veil?" I asked.

"The veil of the Holy of Holies" was his reply. "The veil that separated man from God. Torn in two, from top to the bottom."

I left his house and stepped into the coolness of the evening. My head was spinning. My heart ached for the truth. I wanted to know who this man was. I had to know more, but how?

9

Ruben's Trial

The day was almost gone, and evening was fast approaching. Tabitha was worried that her father had not returned. She knew that soon she would have to push the cheese cart home, but she was not sure that she could.

"Lord, help me," she prayed. "I don't know what's happened to my father. Please, Adoni, please help me."

She sat with her head in her hands and started to cry. Suddenly, she heard a voice she thought she recognized. Lifting her head, she saw Jonathan.

"What is wrong?" I asked. "Are you here by yourself?"

"My father went to the Fortress Antonia to sell some posca to the soldiers and has not returned." Her voice was trembling. "I don't know what has happened to him."

"We must get your cart home first, then we will look for your father. By now your mother must be worried about both of you."

Together they pushed the cart to Tabitha's home. Being next to Jonathan made Tabitha feel so alive. She knew that he was the answer to her prayer, and she quietly thanked Adoni. Once home, they quickly found out from Miriam that Ruben had been detained by the high priest and would face the council in the morning.

"Why was he detained?" I asked.

Miriam explained, "On the first day of the week, Ruben saw and spoke with the Teacher, the One who was crucified. He has been telling everyone that would listen about it ever since. I guess the high priest is not happy about his testimony."

"He saw and spoke with Jesus after he died? That's not possible, is it?"

"Oh yes," responded Tabitha. "My father was with the disciples when Jesus stood in the room with them. Jesus ate broiled fish and talked with the disciples like he always did. My father told people at the market. He was cautioned by an old man to be quiet, but my father wouldn't listen to him."

"Your father's a fool," I said. "Doesn't he realize that it was the council that had Jesus crucified! They don't want to hear about Jesus ever again, much less telling someone that he witnessed the rabbi being alive after they crucified him. My father knows that Ruben attacked me in the marketplace and is upset with me for doing nothing. I don't know who told him. It wasn't me. I told no one. It could only be someone at the marketplace, someone that you know and trust. I'm sure that my father will use this incident as an excuse to punish your father as harshly as possible."

"Jonathan, please help him. You must help him," cried Tabitha.

"Tabitha, this is not Jonathan's problem. Your father has brought this on himself. We must pray that Adoni will intervene and help your father," said Miriam.

"Like he sent Jonathan when I prayed today," said Tabitha. "I know he sent you, Jonathan. I needed you and Adoni sent you. I've been thanking him for you ever since you came."

I marveled at their faith. *Did they really believe that the Lord of Heaven would intervene in such a personal problem? How could they have such faith? Where did it come from? Was it the teachings of Jesus that did this?*

"I have to get home before it gets completely dark," I said. "I will try to return tomorrow." I looked at Tabitha, not wanting to leave. I knew that it would be a sleepless night for her and her mother, and I wanted with all my heart to stay and comfort her. But I also knew that I had to go to see if there was any way that I could help her father. Leaving the house, I pulled my prayer shawl over my head and repeated a psalm of David:

> *Hear my cry, O God; Attend to my prayer. From the end of the earth I will cry to You. When my heart is overwhelmed; Lead me to the rock that is higher than I. For you have been a shelter for me, and a strong tower from the enemy. I will abide in your tabernacle forever; I will trust in the shelter of Your wings.*

Temple Chambers

"Have the prisoner brought in," said Caiaphas.

The day was early. There were about thirty members of the High Council present, and Caiaphas was hoping for a few more members to come in, especially Jonathan's father. He began talking with some of the members quietly about what was reported and what was said the day before when Ruben was questioned.

Finally, Caiaphas turned to the members and said, "This man is charged with spreading false testimony about the crucified rebel Jesus. When questioned yesterday, he denied that the testimony was false, but we later found a bag of Roman coins on him, which would indicate that he has been paid to spread these false rumors. In addition, he knows where the disciples of this rebel are hiding but won't tell us. Where are his disciples?'

"They went to Galilee. That's all that I know. They went to Galilee," Ruben said.

Then Caiaphas asked, "Who paid you those coins to spread false rumors?"

"I got them from the quartermaster at the Antonia Fortress yesterday," was Ruben's reply. It was obvious to all there that Ruben had not slept that night and that the guards had questioned him. It also appeared that they did not like his answers. His lip was split open, his right eye was swollen shut, there was a large cut above his left eye, and he could not walk straight.

"Are you telling me that the Romans paid you to spread false rumors?" asked Caiaphas.

"Honored sir," came Ruben's response, "I was given those coins for delivering posca at the request of Tribune Quintus Magnus. The commander Lucius Atticus was there and gave the authorization to pay me."

"So, you are telling me that my source is lying? That I am lying!"

Ruben didn't answer. He realized that there was no answer to that question. If he said that the high priest was not lying, then the evidence would convict him. If he called the high priest a liar, then he was guilty of disrespect of the ruler of the Sanhedrin. Either way, he was doomed.

"According to our law, a man can be convicted only by the

testimony of two or more witnesses. Do you have two witnesses against this man, Caiaphas?" A man named Joseph asked the question.

Caiaphas spun around to face his new adversary. The other members moved aside, leaving the two standing face to face.

"These are extreme times during which the letter of the law does not always apply," answered Caiaphas.

"So, then I take it that you do not have two witnesses of this man's guilt. I see no reason for this questioning to proceed any further. Turn him loose."

"You do not rule this council," said Caiaphas.

"No," came the reply. "Our laws rule this council. They have been handed down to us for hundreds of years and are not to be put aside by the whim of one man, especially the leader of our Jewish nation. You cannot prove that this man is guilty of anything. I see that he has suffered enough. He should be let loose so that he can return to his work in order to pay his taxes."

"And what of his blood money? Should I give that back to him too?"

"Keep the money if you wish, but let the man go."

Caiaphas looked at the guards and nodded. They untied Ruben and led him out.

Once he was gone, Caiaphas stormed out of the room.

——◆——

We found Ruben on the side of the street. He was leaning against a wall and did not look like he could travel much further, but no one stopped to see about him. Most people did not look in his direction. I knew he needed help.

"Mathias, we have to help him get home," I said. Matthias lifted him from the wall, placed his arms around Ruben, and began to carry him. The sun was hot, and it was apparent that Ruben was in great pain, so it took a while for us to get him home. Once there, Miriam and Tabitha came out and helped Matthias get him into his bed.

"Mathias, get the physician for him," I told him.

"Yes, master. Do you think that he's at home?"

"I hope so. If not, try to find him. Please hurry," I told him.

"Jonathan," interrupted Miriam. "We have no money for a physician. I will take care of his wounds. I can—"

Mathias stopped her. "You can take care of his outer wounds, but he is hurt on the inside. He needs a physician. He may die if he does not get help."

I saw the fear on her face. Tabitha was holding her father's hand. She looked at me, but there was confidence in her eyes like she knew her father was going to be alright. I heard Matthias leave and wondered if he would be back in time.

Then Tabitha said, "We need to pray to Adoni for Father to be healed."

"I really don't think that God has time to deal with this matter nor do I think that Adoni is interested in your father's problems," I told her.

"Jesus said that Adoni is our Father, that he loves us, and that he will help us when we have needs. Jesus healed so many people of all kinds of problems, and he said that we should ask our Father to meet our needs using his name," was her reply. She sank to her knees, lifted her eyes to heaven, and prayed, "Adoni I come to you in the name of your son, Jesus, and ask that you heal my father. I know that his injuries are severe, but I also know that you can heal him."

"If Jesus were here, he would heal your father," said Miriam, "but he's not here. I know that you mean well. . ."

Ruben began to stir. I looked at him. The swelling of his lip and his right eye was no longer visible. I could not see the cut over his left eye. It had disappeared along with his bruises. He sat up without showing any pain.

"How do you feel?" Miriam asked.

"How did I get here? What are you doing in my house?" he said as he pointed at me.

"He brought you home, Father," Tabitha said.

"I found you in the street not too far from your home. Mathias just about carried you. To be honest, I didn't think that you were going to live. I sent Mathias for the physician. How do you feel?"

"I remember now. Someone picked me up just before I passed out. Everything went blank until just a few minutes ago. I heard something about Jesus."

"I prayed for Adoni to heal you in the name of Jesus," answered Tabitha. "Now look at you! You're all well. Adoni healed you."

"Ruben, how do you feel?" Miriam asked again.

"I'm hungry," was his reply. "I have not eaten since yesterday morning, and I am hungry. Do you have anything to eat?"

"Yes, my husband," she laughed because she knew that he was going to be alright. "Would you like to join us for a meal, Jonathan?"

"No, thank you," I answered. "We had something to eat before we left to find your husband."

"You went searching for me?" asked Ruben. "Why?"

"Mathias and I went to the Chamber of Hewn Stones where we knew they would hear your case. I spoke with Rabbi Joseph who told me that you had been beaten last night and released this morning. We took a path to your house, hoping to catch up with you in case you needed our help. I'm glad we did."

"After what I tried to do to you, you were concerned about me?" he asked. "How could you forgive me for what I did?"

"I heard Jesus ask his father to forgive the people who crucified him. If he could forgive those monsters who crucified him, could I do less to you?"

As we were talking, Mathias returned without a physician. I stepped outside to talk to him.

"I was told that Luke has left for his home in Antioch but will return when his business is concluded. I'm sorry, master. Did he die."

"No. He's not dead. As a matter of fact, he has been healed. Completely. His bruises are gone, the cuts are gone, and he is eating a meal as we speak."

"How?" asked Mathias.

"His daughter, Tabitha, prayed for him in the name of Jesus. When she finished praying, I looked at Ruben and saw the transformation. It's amazing. I don't believe it, but I saw it. How can this be?"

Tabitha stepped out of the house. She looked at Mathias and said, "My father would like to speak to you. Would you go to him?"

He stepped into the house and closed the door behind him. Tabitha looked at me and said,

"Thank you. Thank you for all that you have done for us. You are an exceptionally good man; unlike any I have ever known."

"You are so beautiful," I said. The words seemed shallow, so I continued. "I have thought of nothing but you since we met while your mother was attending to my wound."

"Are you saying that you did nothing against my father because of me?" she asked. I nodded. She drew close to me. Her hand reached for my hand, and I felt flushed as it joined mine. My heart was racing. All I wanted to do was to draw her close to me, wrap my arms around her and never let her go, but we were not engaged, and I knew there were many obstacles to prevent that from ever happening.

On the way home, Mathias said, "What I saw is extremely hard to believe. I would not believe it if you just told me. His beating was severe, and his injuries were life threatening. I have seen enough injuries to know."

"I know too," I answered him. It was hard for me to believe too. It was even harder to consider how Tabitha knew that her father would be healed if she prayed in the name of Jesus. There was something here that I did not understand.

"Who was this man? I would have liked to have met this man, Jesus," said Mathias.

"We met him once," I answered. "But now he's dead. We saw him die. I know that he healed me, but he was alive then. How could just using his name bring the same healing power that he used to heal my legs?"

I didn't know if Mathias was going to report all of this to my father, and I was in enough trouble with him already. I was sure that by now he realized that my instance of us discussing my sister's supposed marriage this morning was just a ruse to keep him from being a part of Ruben's trial. My thoughts went back to Tabitha. I smiled. It was nice to know that she feels the same for me that I feel for her. My smile broadened. Our pace quickened. It was getting dark, and the Sabbath was about to start.

10

After the Sabbath

We arrived home just as the shofar sounded Bar'chu, which was the call to worship. The Sabbath had begun. In the house, the mood was cheerful. Every servant was looking forward to a day of rest.

"Shabbat shalom" was my mother's greeting. She wore a beautiful blue veil over her head, the one she wore almost every Sabbath. Her outer garment was of woven linen with tiny ribbons of gold thread along the sleeves. She seemed to be at peace.

The house was unusually beautiful, decorated with fresh flowers from the courtyard. New, colorful pillows were all around, and the smell of roasted meat could be detected from the upstairs dining area.

"Shabbat shalom," I responded.

"Shabbat shalom, Jonathan. It's good that you are with us," said my father. He had been standing next to Mother, but I didn't notice him. The words sounded pleasing, not sarcastic. He looked like he was happy to see me.

"Come," said Mother. "It's time for the Sema." We went upstairs where she lit the Shabbat candles and pulled the smoke to herself. Together we all recited the prayer,

"Shema Yisrael Adonai Eloheinu, Adoni echad Barch shem k'vod malchuto, I'olam va'ed." It was the prayer we recited

every Sabbath. "Hear O Israel, the Lord our God, the Lord is one. Blessed be his glorious name, whose kingdom is forever and ever."

The Amidah blessings followed, then we prayed about our own personal requests. I prayed to know the truth about Jesus, who he was and why he was hated. As we silently prayed, I wondered what Tabitha's prayer requests were. Whatever they were, I was sure that they would be answered. I still wondered how she could have such faith in the crucified Teacher, and I wanted, more than ever, to be with her. The meal continued as we looked forward to a day of rest.

In the morning we went to the temple to join the worship procession celebrating the greatness of the God of Israel and the hope of deliverance from the Romans. By the sixth hour, we were home again. I spent the rest of the day in my room reading scrolls from the prophet Zechariah. He prophesied that the Moshiach, the Messiah, was a humble king full of justice and riding a donkey. He was also a king of war, a hero who fights for us. Did this prophet believe he was both? Was he coming for just the Jews, or was he coming for the gentiles too? Was his purpose restitution and deliverance, or was it the forgiveness of our sins? I slipped my prayer shawl over my head and asked Adoni to reveal his truth to me.

⟳◆⟲

There was a knock at my door. I had just awakened to the smell of fresh bread.

"Yes, who's there?"

"Your father. May I come in?" he asked as he opened the door. He entered my room and sat down. I prepared myself for what was to come, or so I thought.

"Jonathan, I'd like to talk to you. I need to know about some things that are happening in your life."

"What things?" I asked.

"Well . . . let's start with this young girl I've heard about. Is she pretty?"

"No, she's beautiful. But more than that, she has character and a peace about her that I do not understand. She works hard, has faith in God, and respects people."

"Faith in what god?"

"She is a child of Moses," I said, hoping that would satisfy him. "She worships the God of Israel."

"And what about the man Jesus? What does she believe about him?" he asked.

I knew what he was trying to do, but I would not say anything that might condemn her or her family, so I remained silent.

"What do you intend to do about her?" was his next question.

"At the right time, I intend to ask her father to marry her."

"The man who tried to kill you. Who would have succeeded if it were not for Mathias who saved you? You intend to ask him for his daughter? I can't believe this." His voice was getting louder. His temperament was changing. He was getting more frustrated by the minute.

"Think about this family! You would bring her into this house and expect that we would receive her as an equal?"

"Her family is just like us. They are merchants, and we are merchants," I said. My voice was getting more forceful than I intended, but I couldn't hold back.

"They are merchants in a marketplace, I am a merchant

to the world! The fish from my factory in Magdala are sold as far away as Rome. Do not compare me with them," he said as he stood, paced around the room, then sat down again. He took several deep breaths until he seemed to be in control of himself again.

"I guess it is my fault," he said. "I should have arranged for you to be married years ago."

"But who could you have found that wanted to marry a lame son for himself and not for his money?" I said. He glared at me. "You thought that I was destined to be an invalid all of my life. I had no future. My dreams of ministering in the temple were only that, dreams. So, you trained me to be a scribe and a lawyer, knowing that I would have something to do with my life, but that was not enough for me then, and it is not enough for me now. I have legs now, thanks to your rebel Jesus. He gave me hope. He gave me the gift that I needed. It was free. I didn't pay him for it. I didn't even ask for it, but it was what I wanted most in my life. Now I want a family, a wife to love me, to hold me and to give me children, and I want that life with Tabitha."

He looked at me. It appeared that he almost respected me. Then he said, "Jonathan, I'm genuinely concerned about where you are headed in life. You must take inventory of who you are and what you believe. Poverty means that you work hard and do without the things to which you have become accustomed. Be careful in what you believe and do. You could lose your family." He got up and walked out of the room.

I could not tell if he was giving me advice or a warning. Either way it was something to think about. Soon Mathias entered my room and informed me that he and I would be going to Joppa the next day on business for my father. He was instructed to make ready for the trip, to take clothes for three to four days, and to ensure that I was informed of the trip. Then he told me that my sister was visiting again and waiting for me in the courtyard. I instructed Mathias to bring a little bread and some dried figs to the courtyard and was on my way to talk to Shaphrah.

As usual, she was dressed in light-colored clothing of the finest wool. Her hair, what I could see of it, was beautiful and perfectly in place. She smiled when she saw me. We embraced.

"I hear that you've been stirring up trouble," she said.

"You came to straighten me out?" I asked.

We both looked at each other and smiled. Her eyes twinkled, and I knew what she wanted.

"I can't answer your questions," I told her. "I wish I could, but I'm not sure what to tell you about Jesus. Right now, I really don't know who he was."

She stepped close to me like she was going to share a secret when Mathias arrived with a small plate of food. He asked her if she wanted anything, but she declined. He returned to the house. We walked to the fountain with the waterfall.

"What were you going to tell me?" I asked.

She leaned over and whispered in my ear: "He's alive."

"Who?"

"Jesus!"

"And how do you know this?"

"My servant, Zeta, told me that she saw him. She's very reliable. I know her. I know she's telling the truth. Therefore, Jesus must be the Messiah."

"Be careful. Our father just threatened me with poverty because I am in love with a girl whose father says he saw and talked with Jesus three days after his crucifixion. He was arrested and beaten almost to death for telling others what he witnessed."

"Father? Our father? You can't be serious, Jonathan." The smile on her face and the glee in her eyes disappeared. She looked shocked and frightened. "Why? Why would he say that to you?"

"Because he's afraid of what I believe, or what he thinks I believe. He wants to be high priest one day and must stay in the good graces of Annas."

"Why Annas?" she asked.

"Annas has been appointed by the praefectus of Judea as the person who chooses the high priest. They usually serve for a year or two, then he appoints someone else, usually in his family. Our mother is a part of the lineage of Annas, so father believes he has a chance of being high priest at some point. If Annas believes that father's family is a part of the movement to accept Jesus as the Messiah, then he will not be anointed high priest. This is especially important to him."

"More important than his own flesh and blood? I don't believe that, Jonathan," she replied.

"I don't know. It could be that maybe he was just trying to scare me. Maybe. In any case, please be careful who you talk to and share your feelings with. The entire council is set on putting this matter of Jesus to rest. Please listen to me," I begged her.

"I will. Now, tomorrow I will be going shopping at the market. Will you come with me? You can introduce me to your friend."

"Tomorrow I am going to Joppa on Father's business. I will be gone most of the week," I replied.

"Isn't this rather sudden?"

"Yes. I think that this trip is the result of our conversation this morning. He didn't inform me of the trip then, but he sent Mathias later to tell me and get everything ready. Mathias said that we would be gone for the week, so I won't be able to go with you tomorrow." Without realizing it, a broad smile was across my face as I said, "Her name is Tabitha and her family sells cheese on the southern part of the marketplace, and she is beautiful."

Shaphrah smiled. "I will see her tomorrow, and I will judge her beauty." She noticed Abigail coming out of the house and heading for us. She looked like she had been crying. Shaphrah hugged her as she wept.

"Abigail, why are you crying?" she asked.

"Abigail, tell us the problem," I said.

She looked at me and said, "Father just told me that I would not be engaged to Hanel. That he was unable to make the arrangements."

"You want to marry Hanel?" I asked.

"Yes, his father is a very important man," she said.

"Why do you want to marry him?" asked Shaphrah.

"Because it was what Father wanted. I would have been married to an important family. My children would have a strong lineage, and they would be well cared for if I married him. Besides, Father would have been able to get the land next to the factory in Magdala. This would have made Father happy."

"Would it have made you happy?" I asked her.

"Yes," she said. "I met him once and he is very handsome. He was not like the young men in Jerusalem who are full of foolishness and games. We held hands for a while, and I thought he really liked me. I like him. But now it is not to be, and I will be married to one of the fools in Jerusalem."

"I'm sorry," I said. "I thought that Father was selling you to Amir Ben Remiel for a piece of land. I didn't know that you were a part of the negotiations. God will work it out. You will see," I told her. Now I was starting to sound like Tabitha. She looked at me and smiled. I think that she even believed me for a moment. She reached over and hugged me.

Then she asked, "Do you know where Stephen is? He used to come around often, but I haven't seen him in weeks. I could always talk to him when I had problems."

"I don't know," I answered. "But I will try to find him when I get back from Joppa."

11

A Very Fortunate Meeting

The trip to Joppa was a full day's journey by horseback, so we set out before daylight. Father had given me instructions to meet with Clavus Festus Aelius. He was the owner of the pottery shop that made the storage jars used to pack dried and pickled fish from the Magdala factory. He wanted me to negotiate better prices for a larger amount of jars—one and one-half times his usual order. Papers had been drawn up that gave me the right to conduct business in the name of my father.

We arrived just before the twelfth hour and wasted no time by going straight to the house of Clavus. Within an hour, the negotiations were completed, and the contract was signed. Clavus offered me a glass of wine. I declined but mentioned that Mathias might enjoy one as we had been riding all day.

Clavus handed him a glass, poured the wine, and held it up before he said, "So, the big Greek is now a slave. It could have been me instead of you. Luck to you, Nikephoros!"

They touched glasses and downed the wine. Mathias went outside to check the horses. The Roman thanked me for my order and promised I would not be disappointed.

Outside I asked Mathias, "Do you know this man?"

"He was a part of the Roman legion that defeated us. We

fought against each other during the battle, and I wounded him before I was defeated by another soldier."

The next morning the innkeeper brought me a message from my father. The instructions in the message directed me to Caesarea to work out schedules with the boat captains who were shipping the fish from the Magdala factory. I was to see Julius Cassius, a Roman with several ships, and Hiram Igatziu, a Sardinian from Phoenicia who shipped most of Father's goods. Father wanted to know the next shipping dates and where the ships were going. The other information Father was asking for would take several days to secure. He planned on us being there most of the week. I thought about Tabitha and wondered how she liked my sister, Shaphrah.

⊰•⊱

"Husband, do you know when Jonathan will return from Joppa?" Mother asked.

"He will be gone most of the week. I sent word for him to go to Cacsarea to deal with the shipping. Why?"

"Well, I was told by Shaphrah that Jonathan is in love with a young girl named Tabitha, and I wanted to talk to him about her."

"There is no need. He told me all about her and her family. He told me how much he loved her and that he planned on marrying her. I told him that I will not allow him to marry her and disgrace this family. Besides, when I finish with her father, Ruben, he will not be willing to let Jonathan anywhere near his house or his daughter. Jonathan will marry within his clan, and I will find someone for him."

"Joshua bar Gamaliel, I cannot believe what I am hearing. You did not marry within your clan! Why are you so set against this engagement? There must be more to this."

"You are a woman. You do not understand. Stay out of this!" he said as he turned to storm out of the room.

"I am a woman who is a mother. A mother who loves her son. I will tell you this, my husband, if you do not want to lose your son, you need to let him choose his wife. I know him. Interfere in this and you will make him your enemy, and we will lose him."

"We will see," he said.

"And so will he. How long do you think you can keep those secrets? He will find out. And when he does?"

"If he finds out, he finds out. I am his father. I did what I thought was best for him and for this family." He stalked out of the room. When the big, cypress door closed behind him, she began to cry.

⊱⊰

We turned off the Via Maris road toward the Plain of Sharon that cradled Caesarea. It was late in the day, and I could see the sun as a great, orange disk dipping into the Mediterranean Sea. To my right were golden fields of wheat and barley. To my left were green orchards of olives and rows upon rows of grapevines. The city rose out of the land and was surrounded by walls strengthened with sixteen towers and five gates. We headed to the main gate, which was still open. Once inside the city, we quickly found an inn that would care for our horses and offered decent lodging. That evening we enjoyed a proper Jewish meal, after which we retired to our room.

"Mathias, why did that Roman call you Nikephoros?" I asked.

"That is my Greek name. It means 'victory maker.' When I came to your father's house, I was renamed."

"Do you miss your home, Mathias?"

"It has been more than fifteen years since I was home. Most of my friends were either killed or enslaved by the Romans. The city that I lived in was destroyed. I have no home to return to," he replied.

"How did you come to my father's house?" I asked.

"I was defeated in battle by a centurion, Quintus Magnus. Instead of killing me, he made me his personal slave. We were stationed in Jerusalem when one day he took me to your father's house and instructed me that I was now your guardian and nurse, and that I was to obey your father until you became of age, then I was to obey you. It has been a good life."

"What happened to Quintus Magnus?"

"He is a tribune now; he's the Legatus Augusti over the legions in Israel and is governor of Caesarea. His office is here. He serves the praefectus, Pilate."

The next day we were greeted by a Roman soldier who identified himself as Gaius Claudius. He was the beneficiarli to Quintus Magnus. We were asked to accompany him to the Tribune's office. We agreed.

"So, you're the Tribune's secretary," Mathias said.

"Yes and I have heard much of you, Nikephoros. Of all his battle engagements, his defeat of you is his most prized, I believe. He said that you were a great warrior, the descendent of King Antiochus who ruled the Seleucid Empire and that he was lucky to walk away the victor. He is looking forward to seeing you again."

I could not believe my ears. This man who has been

taking care of me for almost fifteen years is the descendent of a king. I understood now what was taken from him and how honorable he is. To become a slave when you are the descendant of a king must be devastating.

As we walked, I could see the city. It was beautiful. The main street was paved and had marbled, white columns on both sides. It led to the amphitheater, which was large enough to hold more than five thousand people at one time. The streets were at right angles to each other, and the homes were mostly small Roman villas. In the center of the large, paved square was the Citadel, which is where we were headed.

The palace that the praefectus lived in was off the main road next to the sea with gardens and statues of current and past Roman emperors. The hippodrome was laid out along the coast and had seating for over half the population of the city. I read the posters that indicated the next race would be in a week. I expected that we were going to be here then. I also wondered what my father was doing to Ruben and his family while I was away.

As we approached the citadel, Tribune Quintus came out to meet us. He was an older man, tall, with a large frame. His curly, gray hair was cut in the Roman style. His face looked like weathered oak with the scars of many battles. Over his red tunic was a leather breastplate with an embossed battle scene. His leather baldric from which his sword hung was trimmed in gold. At the end of it hung his gladius with a brass and leathered handle. He was every bit a Roman commander.

We stopped. Slowly Mathias approached the tribune, then he knelt on one knee and lowered his head. The tribune picked him up, and they embraced. The mutual respect was obvious, but the tribune had another look—one of pride, the pride that a father has for his son.

Finally, the tribune spoke, "Look at you! You've become quite a man. You have honored me by your obedience and have become a trusted ally. Come, let us share a glass of wine together."

With that, we all went inside. In his office, a soldier poured three cups of wine and gave one to me, one to Mathias, and one to Quintus Magnus.

Quintus raised his cup and said, "To truth, honor, and victory."

I really didn't want to drink to his victory, but I thought it best not to mention my feelings at the moment. The wine was the best I'd ever tasted, and I enjoyed it. The tribune called for his secretary, Gaius, and sent him to get Levi bar Alpheus. Then he excused everyone except me from the room.

"Sit down, Jonathan. We have a lot to discuss. First, I would like a report on Mathias. Has he been faithful to you since you've reached the age of assent, or does he still follow your father's orders?"

I replied, "Mathias has become a trusted friend. He listens to and obeys my father when those actions do not violate my wishes. He knows more about me than anyone, and I trust him with my life."

"You know that he belongs to you, do you not?" came the next question.

"Yes. I have read the transfer papers giving him to me as a gift. I really don't understand why."

"Because it was my chariot that ran you over fifteen years

ago. I knew that you would need constant assistance and someone who could help you become the man that you were meant to be."

"As you see, Tribune, I have my legs again. If you want Mathias back, he is yours." My heart broke to say that.

"Mathias is yours to do with as you wish, but I recommend that he stay with you."

I exhaled, and my heart started beating again. I didn't know how I would live without Mathias at my side. There was a knock at the door. Quintus said, "Enter."

A Jewish man entered the room carrying what appeared to be ledgers and scrolls. Some of the scrolls were sealed with red wax, bearing an impression.

"This is Levi bar Alpheus. He is my argentarii, banker, I believe you would call him. Since you are trained in the law, Roman and Jewish, you will be able to understand the information he brings."

I wondered how this tribune knew that I was trained in both Roman and Jewish law.

"What is this about?" I asked.

Levi answered, "The tribune has certain holdings that will be of interest to you since they, in effect, are yours. According to his generosity, you are the legal owner of the salt mine in Cyrenaica of North Africa and the salt production in the Qumram of Judea. In addition, the tribune has given you a villa with servants on the Isle of Cyprus in the city of Nocisia. It is within a Jewish settlement. The villa is a working farm that produces olives and olive oil that is shipped to Rome. I have an accounting of the last 15 years of your ownership, and my bank holds the proceeds from these ventures. The only thing that is missing is the two withdrawals that your father made eight years ago."

He finished his accounting and placed the scrolls and ledgers on the table next to me. Then he said, "Will there be anything else, Tribune?"

Quintus Magnus dismissed him.

"I don't understand," I said. "Why have you done this?"

"I am a very wealthy man. My family is one of the original families of Rome. I own perhaps a hundred times what I have given you. Remember, I did not expect you to walk again. It gave me great pleasure when I found out that you were healed by the man your father calls a rebel. It seems ironic."

"You seem to know a lot about me and my family. How?"

The Tribune grinned. "There is little that goes on in Israel that I don't know about. For example, here are the departure times and destinations of the ships your father sent you to find out. Your new order of containers will be delivered to the factory in Magdala within the month, as scheduled. The ships will be waiting. In addition, in this satchel is the other information that your father wanted you to obtain for him. Now you can get back to Jerusalem and that young girl who has captured your heart."

I couldn't believe what I was hearing. *How does he know so much about me?* I truly didn't know what to say. Slowly, a plan came to mind. I don't remember if I said something out loud or if he was reading my thoughts.

"I cannot thank you enough for your gifts, but I have to go to Magdala first. I must try to arrange a marriage between the son of Amir Ben Remiel and my sister, Abigail."

"I will provide you with an escort to Magdala. You should speak with him there."

"Tribune, I don't know how to thank you. Your generosity exceeds anything I could imagine."

"Now I have a favor to ask of you. Allow me to send you to your inn with an escort so that I might have time with Mathias."

"Of course," I said. "I have a lot of studying to do and can use the time alone to get this done. And again, thank you."

12

The Failed Ambush

Mathias and the tribune left the citadel and began walking toward the main thoroughfare.

"How long has it been since you've tasted authentic Greek food?" Quintus asked Mathias.

"Since I left my home many years ago, but I remember the meals we had as a family. The meal usually started with legume soup and ended with a Gastrin dessert. Unlike these Jews, we had meat at almost every meal—lamb, goat, pork on skewers, but mostly sausages. My mother's recipe for Tzatziki spread was wonderful. I put it on everything," Mathias replied with a smile.

Quintus began to reminisce about his visit to the island of Cyprus and the food he enjoyed while there. They had turned off the main road into an area known as the Greek quarter. Mathias noticed that the street was deserted and that some of the shops were closed. Four men were walking toward them and were acting like they were drunk. They were dressed like Jews. As they were passing, Mathias noticed three other men coming from across the street, looking straight at them. Mathias interrupted Quintus and spoke in the Greek dialect,

"Ambush! Arm yourself, now!"

Mathias reached down and removed the dagger from his boot, then spun around to stab one of the four assailants who had turned on them. Quintus' sword was being withdrawn from the chest of one of the other assailants. Mathias turned back to face the three men who were now running toward them. He threw his knife, which hit the first man in the throat and caused him to fall to the ground. The third man on the left directed his pila at the back of the tribune. Mathias grabbed the pila while kicking the second man in the chest, who fell to the ground. Mathias then spun in a circle removing the pila from the assailant's hands. That maneuver ended with the pila in the chest of the third man.

Quintus had cleanly dispatched his three assailants but not without injury. The man that Mathias had kicked got up and started to run away. Mathias removed the pila from the corpse and threw it at the fleeing assailant, striking him in the right shoulder. He fell to the ground with a scream.

Quintus faced Mathias. "How did you know?"

"Jews never smell like garlic and pork," he said as he grinned. "Let me bandage your wound. Perhaps the meal can wait."

Mathias removed part of his inner tunic and bandaged the left arm of the tribune. Then he walked over to the living assailant and removed the pila. He turned the man over and looked at him.

"You did not bring enough of your friends to do the job," he said.

"I will bring more next time," the wounded man replied.

"For you there will be no next time," said Quintus. "Now who sent you and why?" As he asked the question, he was stepping on the wounded shoulder. The man screamed.

"I like your screams," said Quintus. "You will be doing a lot of screaming before you tell me who sent you, and you will tell me. This I promise. Then you will be crucified. Or you can skip the screams and choose a quick death. The choice is yours. Now talk."

Mathias walked over and removed his dagger from the throat of the dead assailant. He wiped it clean on his clothes. He noticed that the man's coin purse was bulging with coins, so he checked it and the other men's purses. They were also all full of new coins. He pulled the purses from the men's belts.

"Tribune," he said. Quintus turned to look at him. Mathias tossed one of the coin purses to the tribune, who opened and looked at the newly minted coins. Quintus knelt next to the wounded man and said, "I'm going to say two names. You are going to tell me which of the two men gave you these coins. If not, you will die in much pain." He stood up and placed his foot back on the wound of the prisoner and began pressing.

"Gaius Claudius," the prisoner said. "Gaius Claudius gave me the money and instructions to kill you and the Greek."

A squad of Roman soldiers was arriving. They were surprised at the number of men lying dead in the street. Quintus left them with instructions to bring the prisoner to the Citadel and to clean up the mess. Then he and Mathias returned to his office. As they approached the outer door, Quintus withdrew his sword and told the first soldier he saw to get the surgeon on duty. Mathias went first and opened the door. As he entered, Gaius reached for his sword.

"Do you really think that you could be successful with that?" asked Quintus. By that time, his sword was at the throat of Gaius. "Step into my office."

Quintus took Gaius' sword and tossed it on his desk, but

it slid past the edge and fell to the floor. The point sparked as it struck the marble. The sound echoed in an otherwise silent room. A centurion entered the room with Quintus and took up a post in front of the door.

Quintus sat in his chair with his arm still bleeding badly. He threw one of the coin purses on the desk.

"Mistake number one," said Quintus. Gaius bent over and opened the purse. The new coins fell on the top of the desk. "Those new coins were just minted in Rome. Not only do they have the image of Caesar on one side, but they have the new symbol of the Pax Romana. Those coins were received yesterday and have not yet been put into circulation. Besides myself, only two people knew about them—you and the centurion. Now, I know that I didn't give those coins to my attackers, so that leaves either you or the centurion.

"Normally, I would allow the two of you to fight in the arena and let the gods decide who is the guilty one, but you made other mistakes. Mistake number two, you sent those men to kill Nikephoros as well as myself. He did not need my help to kill your friends. Basically, I was in his way as you can see." He held up his arm, which was still bleeding. "It would have taken twice as many men as you sent to kill him and that many again to kill me."

There was a knock at the door. The centurion opened the door to the surgeon, who went straight to Quintus. After unwrapping and examining the wound, he said, "This wound will require stitches."

"Do it" was Quintus' reply. He sat still while the surgeon cleaned the wound and stitched it up. His face showed no pain nor did his expression change. When the surgeon finished, he dressed the wound and told the tribune to see him in the morning to ensure there was no infection. Quintus turned his attention back to Gaius.

"Mistake number three, you hired cowards." The bloodied assassin was dragged into the office. "Is this the man who gave you the coins and the instructions to kill me and the Greek," asked Quintus. A barely audible yes could be heard. Quintus nodded, and he was taken away.

"Now, Gaius Claudius, tell me who paid you to have me assassinated," Quintus demanded. Gaius said nothing.

"Aah, a stubborn little mouse. Tormenting you will be such fun. Or better still, perhaps I will put you in the arena with Nikephoros. After all, you tried to have him killed," said Quintus as he grinned. Then he nodded at Mathias.

Mathias walked over to Gaius and lifted him off the ground using only one hand around Gaius' neck. Gaius' face turned red. His feet were kicking. He grabbed at Mathias' hand as his face began to turn purple. Mathias let him go. He crumpled to the floor, coughing.

"We have just begun, Gaius Claudius," said the tribune. "Have you anything to say before we continue?"

Mathias reached down and picked Gaius up from the floor. He stood him erect, punched him hard in the stomach, then picked Gaius up by the neck and held him off the floor for a few minutes. When he let go, Gaius again crumpled to the floor coughing.

"Don't mind him. He's just having a little fun before we start with the interrogation," said Quintus.

"I am a Roman citizen," said Gaius. "I appeal to Caesar."

"Oh, I'm sure you will see Caesar in the after-life. You can discuss your issues with him then. Right now, you have one choice. Tell me who wants me dead, or you will wish you were dead. This I promise. If you do not cooperate with me, you will be crucified when I am done with you if you are still alive."

"If you kill me, you will never know who is behind this," Gaius said.

"So, how is that different from what I know now? You have been my benefactor in making me aware of the plot. Thank you. But if you are unwilling to tell me what I want to know, you are of no use to me anymore. Your death will be of little consequence to me. The only question remains is how you will die, a quick death on the chopping block or crucified for days."

Mathias picked him up from the floor. "Stand in the presence of the tribune," Mathias said.

Quintus removed his short dagger from its sheath. "Put your hands on the desk."

Gaius refused to comply. Mathias reached from behind him and forced his hands on the desk. Quintus drove the dagger into the right hand of Gaius, pinning it to the desk. He screamed and went to his knees.

"Crucifixion starts with nailing your hands to the cross beam," said Quintus. "Welcome to the beginning of your crucifixion. Who wants me dead and why?"

Gaius remained silent.

"Your dagger, centurion," demanded Quintus. The centurion quickly complied. "His other hand," said Quintus.

"No, No. Please no. I will tell you everything," Gaius begged.

The dagger was removed, and he was seated in a chair facing Quintus. He held his hand, which was bleeding.

"The Primus Pilus, Titus Vinius, is behind the whole

plot. He wants your position and believes that Pilate will give the position to him. He told me that Pilate told him that if anything happened to you, he would petition Caesar on Vinius' behalf."

"And what's in it for you?" asked the tribune.

"I was going to be sent back home to Rome. I would see my wife and daughters again."

"Why did you not come to the tribune with this information instead of participating in this treason?" asked Mathias.

"Because there was money involved," answered the tribune. "Treason can always be purchased. Is that not correct, Gaius?"

⸺⸺◆⸺⸺

I finished going through the legal documents and the accounting of income and investments Quintus gave me. Deeds to the salt mines and the Roman villa were properly recorded and signed by the Emperor. The income from the salt mines was staggering. The accounting indicated that the salt from both mines was sold across most of the Roman Empire, including Magdala. The oil from the villa was traded mostly between Rome and Gaul and brought an unusually high price. With Levi's investments, it seemed that I was as wealthy as my father.

I could not understand why my father told me nothing about these gifts or of the income that they produced for me. He had made two substantial withdrawals several years ago, so I know that he was aware of what the tribune had gifted me. The ownership papers gave him the right of usage until I became eighteen years old.

While I was considering how to proceed with my new-found wealth, Mathias returned. His tunic was bloodied, and there was a small scratch on his right cheek.

"What happened, Mathias?"

He explained the events that took place while he and Quintus were on the way to a Greek inn to have a meal and how they uncovered a plot to kill the tribune.

"Did he find out who was behind it?"

"Yes," he answered.

"So, what happens now?"

"He will set a trap for the individual to expose himself," he said. "I'm not sure what that will be, but you can be sure that he will be successful. He is very resourceful. This is not the first time that someone has tried to kill him. Politics is extremely dangerous, and he has survived where others have failed. I only wish I could stay to help him see it through."

"You can. If the tribune needs you in this endeavor, you have my permission to stay."

"No. Knowing you would have no objections, I offered to stay and help with his plan. He said that everything needed to continue as normal and that I should return to your service so as not to arouse suspicion. He told me that we can leave tomorrow for Magdala with his escort. They will be waiting for us in the morning."

The next morning, I put the ledgers and scrolls into a leather bag and gathered the satchel given to me by the tribune. I gave the bags to Mathias so that they could be secured to my horse, and then we went downstairs. A Roman soldier was waiting for us.

"Tribune Quintus Magnus is waiting for you. Please follow me."

Outside was a contingent of about 80 mounted soldiers.

Standing in front of them was Quintus Magnus.

"I could not let you leave without saying goodbye," he said. Then he reached over and took a beautifully carved wooden box with gold inlays from the soldier standing next to him.

"This is yours, my friend," he said as he handed the box to Mathias. "It is a small token of what you did for me yesterday."

Mathias opened the box. In it was a beautiful gold Triumph Medal on a golden Torc necklace. The medal was a large gold disk embossed with silver scenes depicting the victory of a champion over a lion. The Torc necklace was made of gold strands plated together and bound by a dozen or so silver bands, each with a beautiful stone setting.

"The medal was given to me by Caesar when I foiled an attempt on his life. If you were not with me yesterday, I fear the outcome would have been different. Thank you."

The two men clasped arms and then embraced. The tribune returned to his office. I wondered if I would ever see him again.

13

The Marriage Bargaining

The trip to Magdala was uneventful. Once there, we found the inn that my father always stayed in, and I sent a message to Amir Ben Remiel asking for a meeting.

Shortly after we settled into our rooms, I received an invitation to dine with the Amir that day. I sent Mathias to the marketplace to see if he could find me a suitable tunic since we did not bring such clothing with us. He returned with several linen tunics that were more than appropriate. I bathed, dressed, and was soon on my way to the house of the Amir.

The house had a four-column entrance that opened to a large open hall containing painted panels on the wall and the mosaic of an octopus set in the black and white marble floor. A young man met me who introduced himself as Hanel. He was tall with dark hair. His beard was short. He was well dressed and had an air of confidence about himself.

"You are the brother of Abigail?" he asked.

"Yes. I have heard much about you," I answered.

"How so?"

"Abigail told me of her impressions of you. She said that the two of you have met and that she found you to be very handsome and, how did she say it, not full of foolishness like other young men she knows. I think she liked you very much."

That seemed to please him, and he said, "My father and I would speak with you about this. Please come in."

We entered the atrium, which was exceptionally large. The open roof structure allowed the cedar trees that lined the center to grow very tall. The pool in the center of the open area had four marble walkways leading to it. Servants were lighting lamps due to the failing light. I was led to the far end where Amir Ben Remiel rose to greet me.

"Jonathan, at last we meet," he said. "I have been wanting to speak with you since I heard about your healing at the hands of the Nazarene. You must tell me about the experience..."

"There is really little to tell. I was at the house of Rabbi Simon for the evening meal. The main table was very crowded, so I was being served in the courtyard. I could not hear what was being said in the house, but suddenly Jesus came into the courtyard, stopped, and looked at me. He grabbed my hands and told me to stand. I stood and looked down at my legs that were now straight and supporting me. I was able to walk. By the time I looked up again, Jesus was gone. I hope that satisfies your curiosity."

"You are not like your father. He would have wanted to get to the negotiations, not tell stories. He misses the finer things in life, like making friends and getting to know people. You are different. That is a good thing, I think."

"My father is under a lot of stress. Please forgive him. He was not always like that."

"No," said the Amir. "I remember when he bought out his partners in the fish factory eight years ago. Now he wants to make it bigger. What do you want?"

"I am more interested in the happiness of my sister than in a land purchase," I answered.

"Sit down young man and we will talk. I will ask for more than what the thing you want is worth, and you will try to talk me down. We will act like jackals at each other's throats until a deal is made, or not. This game I have played many times, and I suppose that I am much better at the game than you are, being so young. But I have no desire to take advantage of you so I will ask that you make the first move and give me your proposition."

I sat in a beautiful dark red chair with curved legs like half a circle, and the seat cradled me with comfort. I looked around, thinking of what to say.

"I am here first for the union of your son, Hanel, and my sister, Abigail. As you know, the mohar that my father wanted was the land next to the factory. The Law of Moses suggests a different price, the weight of the bride in gold because you do not live in Jerusalem. My suggestion is that you purchase a small house in Jerusalem and pay a mohar of forty-five pieces of silver.

"Next, I would like to purchase the land next to the factory. You can sell it to me or to my father. Either way he will have use of it for his warehouse. I have papers giving me authority to act in his name in all matters, but if you should only sell it to me, I will pay your price."

He sat there looking astonished. He turned to his son and asked him several questions in a dialect of Aramaic that I did not speak. Finally, he turned to me and said,

"First, let us settle the negotiations concerning the land that you want. I will sell it to you in your father's name for the last price he offered which was 50 talents in gold. As for the other matter, I have a condition."

"Condition?"

"Yes. I have heard about the bravery and skill of your slave, Mathias. His fame goes before him. Such a bodyguard would be extremely useful to me. If you will sell him to me, I will consent to the engagement between my son and your sister. I will pay you 300 talents for him."

"I love my sister and I would do almost anything to ensure her happiness. However, you have asked for the one thing that could never happen. There are many individuals who possess similar skills and can be a bodyguard for you. Mathias has been my legs since I was five years old. He has cared for me as a brother and as a father. I would sooner give my life as to sell Mathias to anyone for any reason. I'm sorry."

"Then I will speak to your father," he said.

"My father cannot help you. The papers of transfer are in my name, not my father's. Mathias is my property and I will not sell him, for any price. I'm sorry, but that is my final word on this matter. I consider these negotiations over." I stood up and turned to go.

Hanel and his father began to clap their hands.

"Wait! Don't go," Hanel said.

"Thank you, Jonathan. Please, please sit down again. I am terribly sorry for putting you through this charade, but I had to know your character. I had to know if your greed extended as far as your father's. Please do not be offended. My son wants more than anything to marry your sister, but I had to know if her whole family was like your father. He is a man who is bent on owning as much of the world as he can. He has little thought for others. He has extremely high ambitions. He seeks the connection to my family for his benefit and cares little for what his child wants. I am sorry for being so harsh in my evaluation of him, but I have known him for almost thirteen years. I ask your forgiveness."

I stood there looking at him. He was right about my father but had no right to speak that way about him to me, especially while I was a guest in his house. I wanted to leave and dissolve all agreements with him, but the love of my sister compelled me to stay.

Slowly I walked back to the chair. Hanel and his father looked at me. I was sure that they could see the anger in my eyes. I waited to speak until I felt that I could control my words and the tone in which I spoke.

"Jonathan," said Hanel. "I ask you, in your sister's name, to forgive my father for what we have done. I can only think of how I would feel if someone said such things about my father. I know that the anger you feel will not last."

I looked at him and said, "You know nothing about me."

"Your sister worships you," he said. "She could not speak of you without the love she has for you showing. She told me of your hardships, your setbacks, and your dreams. Yet, she said, she has never seen you angry. She has never seen you in self-pity. She said that you are always there for her, even in the little things that she made into big things. Her description of you made me envious of you. I told my father not to do this, but he had to find out for himself. Forgive him."

I sat in the chair. Then I told him, "What you said to me about my father should only be said between close friends. I respect my father because he is my father. You should know this."

"We accept your terms for the betrothal, if you are still in agreement," Amir said.

"Are you sure that you want to be connected with such a family?" I asked.

He replied, "You are her family, and I am honored to be connected with you and your sister."

14

WHO ARE YOU?

The following morning, I sent Mathias back to Jerusalem with a letter for my father. It explained that the land next to the factory in Magdala had been purchased and that I had secured the betrothal of Abigail to Hanel. We would leave for Jerusalem within three or four days. We had to conclude the sale of the land before the elders of Magdala and register the upcoming betrothal. Since Amir Ben Remiel would be staying in Jerusalem, I requested a formal meal for the announcement at my father's house.

The next day was the Sabbath. I went to the synagogue in the city, the largest in Galilee. The large stone box altar was carved, depicting scenes from the Jerusalem temple. The tiled floor was beautiful, but the best thing about the synagogue was the sound of worship when we sang to Adoni. It felt good to be in his presence again, and I thanked him for the many blessings he had given me.

On the first day of the week, I went to the fish factory. I quickly saw why my father wanted to expand. It would allow for improved production while reducing waste and spills. I went into the office and checked out the ledgers and accounting. Everything seemed to be correct. The foreman and I stepped off the land, which I just purchased, and discussed building a warehouse. I instructed him to have plans drawn up before my return and estimates for the cost of building the structure. That night I took a walk by the sea. The night air was cool. I decided that I would come back to see the sun rise in the morning before returning to Jerusalem.

It was still dark when I left my room. Outside I could detect the slightest glimmer of light as the sun was trying to rise. It was enough light to guide me on my way. At the factory, many boats were arriving with the night's catch. I wanted to be alone, so I walked northward toward Capernaum. I finally came to a clear area and sat down on a slight rise above the beach. The water was still far away, but I could see most of the beach. The sun was coming up and lighting the sky.

I noticed a lone boat in the water. It seemed to be making its way to the shore. As I looked across the beach, I saw a stranger. He had a fire going and was grilling some fish. I had not noticed him before. I heard him call out to the boat but couldn't understand what he said. He was too far away. Then I saw that one of the men in the boat dove in the water and swam to shore. The boat docked not far from the fire, and the men struggled to haul in their net. As it got lighter, I thought that I recognized one of the men in the group as a disciple of Jesus. They all hugged the stranger. He walked off with one of the men and spoke with him. They were almost close enough for me to hear what they were saying, but I didn't want to intrude. When I looked hard at the stranger, he looked like Jesus.

The sun was up now and shining in my face, so I thought I was mistaken. I watched them for a long while. Eventually, all the men except the stranger walked away to deal with the fish they caught. I watched them go back to the boat. When I looked back, the stranger was gone. I wanted to go down and help those men and ask who the stranger was, but I just sat there.

"Jonathan!"

I heard my name, so I turned to see who was talking to me. I looked up. His face was radiant, his clothes purest white.

"Why do you persist in your unbelief?"

"Who are you?" I asked as I stood up.

"I am the one who healed you."

I faced him. He had a face of the purest love that I had ever seen.

"Who are you?"

"You know who I am," he said.

I closed my eyes to feel his presence. When I opened them again, he was gone. Was he really here? Did I imagine what I just saw and heard? I sat down again, hoping he'd come back. Then I thought about the men on the beach. They were still there. I got up and started running toward them. One of them stopped me.

"Who are you and what do you want?" he asked.

"My name is Jonathan. I just spoke with a man who looked like the Teacher that was crucified. I saw him talking with you. Who was he?"

A man named John approached me. He looked at me and said, "The master appeared to you and talked to you?"

"I'm not sure. I think he did, or maybe I dreamed it. I was at his crucifixion. I watched him die. How could he be alive?"

John smiled. "He came to you for a reason," he said.

"What reason? Why did he come to me?" I asked.

"Only you know the answer to that," he said as he joined his friends on the boat, and they sailed out to sea.

15

WHAT ABOUT STEPHEN?

Hanel, his father, and their family arrived the day before I got to Jerusalem. They were staying in Herod's palace and had met with my father to ensure that the arrangements in the Ketubah were agreeable. When I arrived the next day, I was treated as a hero. My sister Abigail ran to me, grabbed me, hugged me, and kissed my cheek.

Then she whispered in my ear, "Thank you. I knew you could do it. Thank you."

"I hope that you are happy with him and that you have many children. I don't know him that well, but I got to know his father. I know that Hanel loves you and will treat you with respect."

My father was not home, so I asked to speak with my mother privately. We went into my father's study.

"Mother, did you know about the tribune's gifts to me?"

"So, you met Quintus Magnus. Yes, I know what he did for you."

"Why did you not tell me?"

"Because your father forbids me to tell you."

"Why? How long did he plan on keeping this a secret?"

"That you must speak to your father about. What else do you know?"

"What else should I know?" I demanded.

"Jonathan, please do not ask me about these things. Do not put me between you and your father."

"Mother, look at me. I am your son. I have a right to know everything that concerns me. Have I not proven my loyalty to my family by making the arrangements Father could not? I am my father's son. All that he has is mine. That's the law. I can claim my inheritance now. Right now. But I have no need to. Thanks to Quintus, my financial future is settled. Mother, I love you and I respect my father. But right now, I feel that he has used me, my accident, and my healing to his benefit, not mine. Shaphrah is settled wisely, Abigail will be settled well, so all I worry about now is you."

I reached for her and drew her close to me as she was crying. I was asking too much of her.

"I will speak to Father. I will not put you between us. I know that you must obey him."

"Be careful, my son. Be careful," she said as she looked up at me. "I don't think that you know the true nature of your father's ambition."

We rejoined the rest of the family. The house was being cleaned, and the meal was being prepared for tonight's celebration. My sister Shaphrah was there with her husband and child. I wanted to tell her of my experience at the Sea of Galilee, but I knew that we couldn't get alone because she was helping Abigail to get ready for tonight. Tomorrow would be soon enough.

There was somewhere I had to go. I found my mother and told her that I was going out but would be back before the guests arrived.

"Where are you going?"

"To find Stephen," I answered. "As a good friend I

thought that he might rejoice with us over Abigail's good fortune. Besides, I promised Abigail that when I returned from Joppa, I would find him and invite him over. She wanted to talk with him."

I left the house. It wasn't long before I discovered where Stephen was staying. When I got there, several men tried to stop me from entering, but Stephen called my name, and they let me pass. I went in to find Stephen along with several others. I knew Philip, Timon, and several others. I thought that I recognized several of Jesus' disciples. Stephen and I went to the roof.

"I've come to invite you to our house to celebrate with us. Abigail is to be engaged to Hanel, the son of Amir Ben Remiel. The ceremony is tonight at the evening meal."

"I'm sure that you recognize many of the men in the house," he said. "We are all here because we have something in common. We're in hiding because . . ."

"You all saw Jesus after his crucifixion," I said to him.

"How did you know? Well, I guess everybody knows, that's why we are being hunted by the High Council," he said. "He is alive. Jesus rose from the grave just like he said he would."

"I know," I said.

"How do you know?"

"I saw him in Galilee, by the sea. He appeared to me, called my name. At least I think he did. It may have been a dream."

"So, you're one of us! You know who Jesus is!"

"Wait a minute, Stephen. I'm not sure what I believe yet. I have more questions than answers right now. One of his disciples, John I think, told me that Jesus came to me for a reason. When I asked what reason, he said that only I knew the answer to that. I don't. I don't know why he came to me or even if he came to me. I mean I've seen things that I did not understand. I saw a man who was savagely beaten, almost dead, be healed when his daughter prayed for his healing in the name of Jesus. I know Jesus' power. He healed me, but that was when he was alive. To pray in his name after his death and have such a miracle happen is, well, I don't understand."

"You mean Ruben," Stephen asked. "What happened to him is not fair."

"What happened to him?"

"Someone was able to take all of his farm animals from him. Without his animals, he cannot make the cheeses that he sells in the marketplace. He'll lose his farm to taxes."

"Stephen, I have a favor to ask. If I give you the money can you replace the animals taken from Ruben's farm? No one can know that they came from me." I tossed him my leather purse. He looked in it.

"With this much money, I could purchase his whole farm. I will be glad to help you. Philip and I will go as soon as you leave. I don't know if I can make Ruben take the animals, but I will try."

"Tell him that they came because of Tabitha's prayers. Use the rest of the money to help those in hiding from the High Council, and may God go with you."

When I got home, I went to my room to change and prepare myself for the evening's festivities. Mother followed me.

"Did you talk to him? Is he coming?" she asked.

"No, Mother," I answered. "He has other commitments, but he sends his love and congratulations to Abigail."

"Is everything else okay?"

"You look beautiful, Mother. You will shine tonight even brighter than Shaphrah," I told her, but that did not deter her.

"Jonathan, is everything else okay?" she persisted.

"Yes, Mother. Everything is fine. Now I must prepare for our guests."

I don't think she was convinced, but she left my room. I pulled my prayer shawl over my head and recited one of David's psalms,

O God, you take no pleasure in wickedness; you cannot tolerate the sins of the wicked. Therefore, the proud may not stand in your presence, for you hate all who do evil. You will destroy those who tell lies. The LORD detests murderers and deceivers. Because of your unfailing love, I can enter your house; I will worship at your Temple with deepest awe. Lead me in the right path, O LORD, or my enemies will conquer me. Make your way plain for me to follow.

I changed my clothes and joined the others. Hanel and his family had just arrived and were warmly welcomed into our home.

Once all the necessary introductions were made, Hanel said to my father, "I come to your house for you to give me your daughter, Abigail, as my wife; I am her husband from this day and forever."

They were given one cup of wine to drink together to seal the bargain. Everyone congratulated them and their parents. Abigail seemed incredibly happy. After the meal, Father and

I, along with Hanel and his father, went into the study to conclude the Ketubah contract and set a date for the wedding feast. All was agreed upon, and everyone signed the contract. We returned to the others, and I noted that my mother was nowhere to be found. I went looking for her and found her out in the courtyard. She was crying.

"Mother, why are you crying? Abigail seems happy. I've had a long talk with Hanel, and I know that he will respect her and take care of her," I said. "You should be rejoicing for her."

"For her I rejoice; for you I weep," she answered me.

"Why, Mother?

"I am afraid for you, afraid to lose you."

"Enough of that for now. You have guests in your house that you must attend to. Dry your eyes and return to the festivities. We will talk of this another day. Tonight is for Abigail," I said.

"Yes, you are right. I must think of her first," she said and turned to go back to the house.

"And Mother, you will never lose me," I said with a smile on my face.

The next morning, I was summoned to my father's study. I brought Mathias with me.

"Welcome back," my father said. "I'm proud of you for this accomplishment. It seems that I am not the only one in this family with a head for business. But I must ask you, how did you accomplish this deal and so quickly?"

"I received encouragement from Tribune Quintus Magnus. He sent me to Magdala with an escort of Roman soldiers and assured me that I would find Amir Ben Remiel at his home there. The rest was easy as Hanel really wanted to marry Abigail," I answered, hoping he would take the bait that I set for him.

"So, you met Tribune Magnus. Did someone introduce you to him?"

"Oh no, Father," I answered. "He knew that I was coming before I ever got there. He had all of the paperwork that you requested ready before he ever spoke to me." I handed him the satchel the tribune gave me, then continued, "He also knew Mathias, or should I say Nikephoros, before he knew me. As a matter of fact, Mathias saved the life of the tribune the day of our meeting."

"Mathias. This is true? Tell me about what happened."

Mathias recounted the incident with a great deal less credit than I would have given him. When he was finished sharing what happened, my father sat there scratching his beard, not knowing what to say next. So, I helped.

"My meeting with the tribune was before the assignation attempt. He had his banker, Levi bar Alpheus, give me an accounting of my holdings. You knew about those, didn't you?"

Father looked at me, then spoke to Mathias, "You can leave us now, Mathias."

Mathias looked at me. When I nodded, he left, and I waited for my father to make the next move.

Father watched Mathias leave, then turned to me. "What are you implying, Jonathan?"

"I'm not implying anything," I told him, trying not to get him upset. "I'm a little curious as to why you threatened me with poverty the day before I left when you knew that Quintus Magnus had gifted me a source of income. In addition, there are other giftings including a villa on the island of Cyprus that is self-sufficient. And I am wondering why you kept this a secret from me. Were you ever going to tell me?"

"Jonathan, you are my son. Everything I have is yours, and everything you have is mine. I did not feel that the time was right for me to explain what the tribune gave you. I was concerned about your dedication to Adoni and the infatuation you have for this young girl. I know. I know. Maybe I was a little short sighted about you and the direction you were headed in, but I had your best interest at heart."

"Father, first, everything you have is mine. That is the law. However, everything that I have is *not* yours. Now that I have reached the age of assent, you are no longer able to access my holdings. You have not acted in my best interest. You withdrew money from my holdings to buy out your partners in the fish factory eight years ago. You have not paid that back. In addition, you do not pay for the monthly salt you purchase from my mine. The . . ."

"Let me tell you something," he interrupted as he stood and walked toward where I was sitting. "You are my son and will be obedient to me, or I will have the council deal with you. Do you understand?"

"Like you had the council deal with Ruben? Like you had Ruben's animals taken from him, no doubt on some trumped-up reason," I responded.

He stopped. He put his hands behind his back and began walking back and forth. I could tell that he was trying to get control of himself.

"Father, I am your son. The love I have for you is complete, and I respect you as my father. I don't care that you used the money from my holdings to secure the fish factory. It was the best thing you could do for our family. My salt that you use each month increases your profit, which is also good for this family. My problem is that you have done this without my knowledge or consent. You failed to tell me of the blessings given to me, and yet you threatened me with poverty to control me. You should know me better, Father. You really should know me better."

I stood and left the study. He was silent as I walked out. I quietly closed the door behind me. Mother was standing waiting at the door. She looked at me. I walked over to her and kissed her cheek, then went to my room. I crossed over to my desk and sat down. I began tapping the desk with my fingers. I didn't know if I was mad at what my father had done, or if I was happy to confront him finally. There was a knock at my door. I assumed it was my mother, so I said, "Enter."

Shaphrah quickly entered and closed the door. She walked over to where I was sitting, bent down, and kissed me. Then she pulled a chair close to me and said, "How can I thank you for what you have done for Abigail, and for Father?"

"There's no need to thank me, she's my sister too. As for Father, well, the factory needed the extra space. I'm sure that he'll put it to good use." I looked at her intently. I knew that she wanted to talk about Jesus, but I wasn't ready to tell her everything, so I asked her, "What did you think of Tabitha when you met her. I would really like to know."

"You're right. She is beautiful and so graceful. I introduced myself to her as your sister and told her that I had heard a lot about her. You should have seen her blush. She asked if you were at home, so I explained about your trip to Joppa and that you would be gone for a week or more. She said that she would pray for your safe return, and then her mother called her to help with the customers. I like her very much."

"I'm afraid that Father doesn't share your opinion of Tabitha and her family," I said. "He's had her father thrown into jail. Now he's taken all of their animals from them, which is their source of income. He's doesn't want me to marry her and says that they are not our equals."

"Why would our father do that?"

"There is no political gain for him in my marrying Tabitha. He probably wants me to marry someone's daughter who is in the Sanhedrin so that it will improve his position on the council," I said. "But let's not talk about Father. I have some information that I think you ought to know."

"What?" she asked.

"When I was in Magdala, I walked out by the sea early one morning. There I saw a boat with the men who were the disciples of Jesus fishing. As they were coming toward the shore, they threw out their nets and caught an astounding amount of fish. Then I noticed a stranger on the beach. I thought that I recognized him but wasn't sure because the sunlight was in my eyes. I watched them for a long time, then the men who were on the boat went back to deal with the fish they had caught.

"I hadn't noticed that the stranger left. I sat there and watched them until I heard someone call my name. When I turned to see who called me, I saw Jesus. I asked him, 'Who are you.' He said he was the one who healed me. So, I asked him again, 'Who are you.' He replied, 'You know who I am.' In his presence there was such peace that I closed my eyes. When I opened them again, he was gone."

"Jonathan, have you shared this with anyone?"

"I shared it with Stephen, but I do not want this shared

with anyone else. Please, do not tell anyone about this. Do you understand?"

"Why? This proves that he is the Messiah, doesn't it?"

"This proves nothing. For all I know it could have been a dream. I ran down to the beach to talk to the men that were with him. One of the men told me that the 'master,' as he called him, came to me for a reason. When I asked him what reason, he answered that only I knew the reason."

"How strange," she said.

"Shaphrah, listen to me. The High Council will stop at nothing, absolutely nothing, to ensure that this Jesus of Nazareth remains in the grave. Do not repeat what I have told you, to anyone. I would hate to be the cause of my most beautiful sister being jailed."

"They wouldn't. Father wouldn't let them."

"Yes, they would, and Father might be the one who sends them. They are frightened of this man, Jesus. Frightened men do extremely dangerous things."

"So, do you believe in him, I mean as the Messiah?" she asked.

"I don't know what I believe. My heart says one thing, and my learning tells me something else. I'm just not sure."

"Perhaps you should follow your heart," she said with a smile. Then she moved to the door, stopped, and looked back at me.

"How can I help you?" she asked. I could see the worry in her eyes.

"Be safe and pray to Adoni for me, that I might know his will in this matter."

When she opened the door, Mother was standing there.

Mother looked at us and said, "Your grandfather will be

in Jerusalem for the feast of Pentecost. He will be staying with us during the celebration. You both should know that your father is not happy that he is coming."

"Why?" Shaphrah asked.

"Your grandfather does not approve of your father's ambitions, nor does he approve of the methods that your father is using to accomplish those ambitions," she answered.

"I don't understand," said Shaphrah.

"You know all you need to know. I mentioned these things only to make you aware of the problem," said Mother.

"Do you know when he will arrive?" I asked.

"He will be here the day before Pentecost. He is bringing his first fruits from this year's crop. I understand they had an exceptionally good year," Mother replied. Then she turned and walked away.

Shaphrah looked at me and said, "Do you know what's going on?"

"I know that Grandfather has not seen me since my healing. He has not seen me walk, or run, or ride a horse. He has not seen the smiles in my sisters' eyes or the wonder on my mother's face when they look at me. I'm sure he does not know about Abigail's betrothal." I smiled as I was talking. "I wonder if he remembers all those nights during times of Pentecost when he and I studied the Torah all night and into the morning. He taught me everything that I know about the Law. Such wonderful memories."

The nurse brought Shaphrah's son to her for a feeding. She and the nurse went upstairs. I decided that it was time for me to talk to Ruben so I called for Mathias who came quickly, and we headed for the marketplace.

16

Grandfather's Pentecost

Grandfather arrived earlier than expected. I was in my room thinking of how to tell my father that I would soon be engaged to Tabitha when I heard Grandfather's voice booming through the house, calling my name.

He opened the door to my room and said, "Here you are. I've been looking for you, Jonathan."

I stood up and embraced him. I was a little taller than he was, but his huge arms wrapped around me. His beard was long and gray like his hair, and there were tears in his eyes as he looked at me.

He stepped back and said, "So, it's true. Jesus of Nazareth did heal you. Praise God. Praise his holy name. He has done great things!"

"Blessed be his name, forever," I responded, and he hugged me again. "It's so good to see you, Grandfather. I have much to tell you."

"We will have time while I'm here," he said. "Would you mind my sharing this room with you while I am here?"

"It would be my honor," I said. "And maybe we can renew our old tradition of studying the Torah all night. Do you remember?"

"Yes, I remember. Those were great times," he responded.
Mother appeared at the door.

"Martha, it's good to see you. I know that I'm a day early, but when I heard that Jonathan was healed and could walk, I couldn't wait to see him. I hope you don't mind."

My mother smiled, but I knew that she was not looking forward to the conflict that would develop between her husband and his father.

"You are always welcome in our house. I have a place prepared for you that I hope you will find comfortable," she said.

"I was going to stay with Jonathan."

"I think that you will find this place quiet and more private than staying with Jonathan," she said.

"Of course," Grandfather said. Then he turned to me and said, "Is Mathias still with you?"

"Yes," I told him. "I will send him to get your things."

"We'll talk later," said Grandfather. He followed my mother to the room that had been prepared for him.

Abigail came into my room, "Was that Grandfather's voice I heard?"

"Yes," I said, "Mother brought him to the guest room." She ran off in that direction. I knew that I would see him later. When Mathias was finished helping Grandfather, we left to find Stephen. I had to know what he knew about this man called Jesus.

At the evening meal, Abigail asked Grandfather, "We miss you, Grandfather. Why did you move to Hebron?"

"I got tired of being an absentee farmer and of living in Jerusalem to teach young men the finer points of the Law," he said. "After I make my offerings to the Lord at Pentecost, I will stay a week or so to be with my family and to visit with some old friends, then I will return to my home in Hebron. You and your husband are welcome to come visit. We have more than enough room and your grandmother would love to see you."

"Why did she not come with you to Jerusalem?" she asked.

"There is work to be done after harvest. There is always work to be done at the farm, and your grandmother would have no one else oversee it but herself. Ask your father, he remembers."

"I remember that we are of the tribe of Levi, and it is our position to be priests unto the Lord, not farmers," was Father's response.

"Yes," said Grandfather. "And I ministered in the temple for over twenty years and taught young men the ways of the Lord and the meaning of the law as written in the Torah. But now, Jerusalem has become too corrupt. Ambitious men have allowed their greed to pervert the law and the prophets for their own gain. They have become a contradiction to all that I taught. Your mother and I are at peace in Hebron. Let's leave it at that."

I could feel the tension building between them, and I knew that my mother was worried, but the next day was Pentecost. The feud between them was put aside for the feast day. After supper, Grandfather retired to his room. As I was about to leave, Father called me to his study. I walked in and sat down in a small leather chair. Father entered behind me, closed the door, and sat in a chair next to me.

"We did not finish our last discussion," he said. "I know that you were upset with me. I know that you think that you love that young girl, but you will see in time that I am correct in this matter. I have chosen someone else for you to marry. She is a very pretty, young girl whose family is of our tribe.

She will make you a good wife. In time you will see that marriage can be a steppingstone."

"Father, this discussion is pointless. I have already asked Tabitha's father for permission to enter a betrothal with his daughter. Soon it will be settled, and we will be husband and wife." I could see that he was getting angry.

He got up and walked around me. "Didn't I tell you that you could not marry that girl? She is not the one that I have chosen for you. She will never be a part of this family! Do I have to bring this matter to the Council?"

"Father, I am tired of this debate," I said calmly. "I am of the age now where you can no longer demand that I obey your wishes, especially about marriage. The Council has no authority in this matter. You know this, so why do you threaten me with idle words? I do not share your ambition of being Chief Priest nor do I have any desire to be a part of the Council. It is my life now, and I will plot my course. I respect you, but I will not be a part of your ambition. My desire to marry Tabitha will not diminish, and I would hope that you would see her for who she is to me and not for the political benefit she could bring to you. I have spent fifteen years of my life in pain, but now I am free. Please, Father, don't make me choose between my future and my family. You will not like the choice I make."

I stood up and looked in his angry face. I reached out to embrace him, but he turned away. He walked over to his desk.

"Is there anything else you wanted to speak with me about," I asked.

"No," was his response. "You may go."

The beginning of Pentecost brought my grandfather to my room. He brought several scrolls for our overnight study. I had spent the day in physical training with Mathias. Then I enjoyed a hearty meal and a bath. I was ready for a sleepless night of listening to my grandfather explain the buried meanings hidden in the Torah, or so I thought. First, he wanted to know about my life since my healing. I started with the story of my healing by Jesus and how my father tried to convince me that it was because of my ritual purification at the pools in Magdala. Next, I told the story of how I met Tabitha when her father attacked me while I was going to the trial of Jesus and what Miriam told me about my father's treatment of her husband's brother. I told Grandfather of what I saw at Jesus' trial and what my father said to Pilate.

"Are you sure these words came from your father?"

"Yes, I confronted him about what he said when we were at the city of Tiberius. He acknowledged that they were his words."

"My foolish son. Did he not know who they were crucifying? I have taught him the scriptures, their meanings, and the future events of which the scriptures speak. He had to have known."

"Known what, Grandfather?"

"Who it was they condemned, but that is a discussion for another time. I still want to know what else has happened in your life since your healing."

I was stunned. Did Grandfather know something about Jesus of Nazareth? I wanted to pursue this topic. I wanted to know what he knew or what he thought about Jesus, but out of respect, I continued telling him about the things that happened to me. I told him about my trip to Joppa and why I thought Father sent me on that trip. I told him about my meeting with Tribune Quintus Magnus and showed him all the documents given to me by his banker.

Grandfather looked over the documents very carefully and said, "Jonathan, these documents are authentic and have been registered with the Roman government. Your legal right to these gifts cannot be questioned. You are an extremely lucky and a very wealthy young man. Does your father know about these?"

"He not only knows about these, but he withdrew money from the salt mine account to buy out his partners in the fish factory in Magdala eight years ago. In addition, he never told me about these gifts until he knew that I was aware of them."

"I wondered how he managed to buy out the fish factory," said Grandfather. "I'm just surprised that he didn't try to take the whole amount. Now tell me about Tabitha and about your experience in Magdala."

"Tabitha? She's beautiful, Grandfather. She moves with such grace and has a voice that sounds like a nightingale. Her faith in God is exceptionally strong. She has good sense and loves her mother and father. She's about fifteen and is an only child, which might explain why she's not married. I've asked her father to consider my engagement to her. He has not answered yet. I'm troubled by the possibility of marrying her even though I know that she loves me as I love her."

"Why is that, Jonathan?"

"The law says to honor your father and mother. My father does not want me to marry Tabitha. He disapproves because she cannot bring any benefit to his political ambitions.

He has chosen someone else. Someone I don't even know. He says that the marriage will be a steppingstone."

"For you or for him?" asked Grandfather.

"I don't want a steppingstone; I want a wife. Someone to love me, to believe in me, and to have my children."

"I will speak to him," said Grandfather. "Now tell me about your meeting the Amir Ben Remiel."

"The meeting was very productive, although I found their customs of negotiating a little different from our strict Jewish rules. He was very blunt in his evaluation of Father and shared things with me that probably should have been left unsaid. We negotiated quickly and with honor. I found that I started to like his son Hanel, and I respect him. As for Amir Ben Remiel, I will reserve judgment."

"He is a Jew on his mother's side, the son of a wealthy Syrian Arab who took a Jew for a wife and converted to Judaism. He wrote me a letter the day he arrived in Jerusalem. It was because of this letter that I learned of your healing. Your father never let me know. The Amir and I are friends. He wrote to tell me that he was proud to be connected with my family and how much he respects you. Do not take his respect lightly. He is an immensely powerful man in Herod's court."

There was a knock at the door. Mathias entered with bread, dates, and some honey. He placed them down on a small table along with cups and some goat's milk.

"I thought the two of you might be hungry since it is near morning," he said as he left the room.

"It seems we have spent the night away with very little study," said Grandfather.

"It would seem that way," I said. "But before you go, could

you please tell me what it was that my father should have known about the man they condemned."

"We'll talk about that later. I promise. Now I must go to prepare myself for the offering I am making today at Pentecost. I must get my things together and get to the pool to be washed seven times. I much prefer to go early than late." He got up and left my room. I laid down with a cup of milk in my hand and fell asleep.

17

My Decision

When I awoke, it was afternoon. Mathias went with my grandfather to help carry the grain offering and the other items he was dedicating to the Lord, so I decided to see if I could find Stephen. I was unable to find him the last time I looked for him, so I went to a different part of the old town. A mutual friend told me where to go. When I got there, there was a tall man with Stephen. I recognized him as the man I talked to by the Sea of Galilee. As they approached, the man smiled.

"I remember you from Galilee," he said.

Stephen spoke, "This is John. He is one of the disciples of Jesus. He was with him from the beginning."

"So, do you know the reason he appeared to you?" asked John.

"No," I said.

"Jonathan, why do you persist in your unbelief?"

"That's what he asked me when he appeared to me."

"What else did he say to you?"

I thought a minute, then said, "He said that I knew who he was."

"He loves you, Jonathan. He died for your sins. All you have to do is believe. The law was given by Moses, but God's unfailing love and faithfulness came through his Son, Jesus, who is the Christ. He has revealed God to us. When you believe, you are reborn, not a natural birth, but a birth that comes from God."

Stephen sat listening. His eyes were bright, and he seemed to soak up every word from his disciple friend. I thought how much this man sounded like Nicodemus when I talked to him. But something still troubled me.

"I don't understand the cross. Why was he subjected to such pain and suffering? I was there. I saw what they did to him."

"Jonathan, as sinners we all deserve the cross. The cross was his statement of love for us. He submitted to it freely. I was with him the night they came for him. When he asked them who they wanted, they said they wanted Jesus of Nazareth. He answered, 'I AM he,' and they all fell to the ground. They had no power over him, but he submitted to God's will so that you and I, all people of the earth, would be able to be reconciled to Yahweh our Father. That was his purpose in coming. He did not come to drive out the Romans or to rescue the Jews. He came for the forgiveness of sin, our sin."

The scholar in me wanted to debate. The lessons I learned from childhood stood like an iron door blocking the love that I had for the man who healed me and so many others. My heart knew who he was, but my reason did not want to yield. I thought of Tabitha and her childlike faith. She has no doubts about Jesus. I knew that I had to make a decision, but first I had to talk to Grandfather. He knew something, and I had a feeling that I needed to hear it.

"Jonathan, God has made Jesus to be both Lord and Messiah, and as you know, has raised him from the dead.

There is salvation in no one else. God has given no other name under heaven by which men can be saved!"

I turned to leave, but Stephen stopped me.

"Jonathan, don't go. You must believe. This morning something wonderful happened to us. We were all in a room praying. There was a rushing wind, and we were all baptized in the Holy Spirit. We spoke in languages we didn't even know. A large crowd gathered, and Peter preached about Jesus. Thousands repented and were baptized in the name of Jesus. These were Jews from Mesopotamia, Phrygia, Pamphylia, Egypt, and even from Rome. They believed. I know you believe; I know you do."

I reached over and grabbed Stephen. I hugged him, then said, "Stephen, I will be back." I returned home.

When I got home, Grandfather was waiting for me in my room. He was sitting at my desk with a small scroll in his hands.

"Jonathan, I'm glad you're home. I wanted to give you something that I've kept for you. As my first grandson, I purchased a small area of land close to Bethlehem in your name. This was to be a wedding present to you when you got married, but somehow, I believe that right now is the time to give it to you. I would appreciate you not sharing this with anyone."

He handed me the small scroll. I examined it. It represented a plot of land about eight miles west of Bethlehem with small streams on two sides.

"It is currently being rented to sheep farmers," Grandfather told me. "The rent is not very much, but it pays the taxes. It can be sold to the farmers for more than its value."

"Thank you, Grandfather. Of course, I will not share this with anyone if that is your wish."

"It is," he said. "Your grandmother and I had hoped that you would settle there, but now I know that will not happen. If I were you, I would go to that villa on the Isle of Cyprus. Cyprus is a beautiful place. I've been there many times. You would be at peace there."

"Can there be peace in this world?" I asked.

He smiled. "I heard a man today who spoke of the peace of God. A man could achieve it, he said, by believing that Jesus was the Christ, and that he would forgive our sins and make us right with God. He was very convincing. Many went with him to be baptized. I almost went myself."

"Why didn't you?"

"That is another story, but we don't have time right now. Your mother will be calling us for the evening meal shortly. We will talk in the morning if that's all right with you."

He got up to go. He looked tired. "Can I help, Grandfather," I asked.

"No, no. I'm fine. Just tell your mother that I may not be there for the evening meal."

Grandfather woke me early. He had some goat's milk and cheese along with some fresh bread. He set the cheese and bread down on the table next to me.

"Eat something. It will make you strong." He sat next to my desk and handed me the milk after I had taken a bite of bread. When I was through eating, he stood up, locked my door, then pulled a chair next to my bed. "What do you think of your talk with Nicodemus?" was Grandfather's question.

"It gave me a lot to think about. I was surprised to hear that he now believes that Jesus was the Messiah and that he considers himself a follower," I answered him.

Grandfather looked at me and said, "I am as he now is."

"What do you mean? Are you a follower of Jesus also?"

"Yes. I was baptized by one of his disciples in the Jordan several months ago. I would appreciate you not telling your father about this news. Your father and I do not have the same interests in our relationship with Yahweh."

"Grandfather, there's something I have to tell you. Since being able to walk, I have listened to what the man Jesus taught. I was there at his crucifixion. I discovered who my father really is and how he uses his power to hurt others for his personal gain. I'm not proud of him, but I still love him. I listened to Nicodemus and searched the scriptures to find if Jesus was who he claimed to be. But the most convincing thing that I have is that he appeared to me after he was crucified, at the sea of Galilee. He said that I knew who he was. Now I find out that you have accepted him as the Messiah."

"He appeared to you after he rose from the grave? He has a plan for you, Jonathan."

"Everyone keeps telling me that, but I don't know the reason he appeared to me!"

"You will in time. First you must surrender to him, repent, and be baptized. Go back to the disciples. They can help you. As for myself, I must go with your father to the High Council meeting today. It seems that they arrested some of Jesus' disciples yesterday, and they are going to bring them before the Council this morning."

"What did they arrest them for?"

"Healing a man who couldn't walk. He was lame from his mother's womb, and the disciples healed him. So, they arrested the men who healed him. I'm sure that makes perfect sense to somebody."

⬥

It was late morning before I was able to find Stephen. He was with Philip, in the old city of David, debating some men from the Synagogue of the Freedmen. I listened to their arguments, but they could not stand against the ones presented by Stephen. Some of the men were getting angry, but their leader invited Stephen back for another discussion, and he agreed. When he turned, he saw me. He looked happy to see me.

"Jonathan! You've come back," he said. "Did you find out what you wanted to know?"

"Yes," I answered. "And I know who Jesus is. He is the Messiah, the Son of God, and he came to die for my sins. So I no longer persist in my unbelief." Stephen grabbed me and hugged me so tight that I thought he was going to squeeze the life out of me.

"Have you been baptized?" asked Philip.

"No."

"Let's go now to the Pool of Siloam so that you can be baptized," Stephen said.

On the way there, I asked about Ruben and Tabitha. I hadn't seen them for a while and was concerned about them. Philip said they were fine and that they had been baptized about a week ago. Stephen told me that Tabitha had asked about me and shared that she missed me. I resolved to go see them after I was baptized.

Suddenly, there was a hand on my shoulder. I turned to see Mathias. I stopped.

"Master, I've been searching for you," he said. "I have a message from your mother."

He handed me a small scroll. I opened it and read:

Be careful what you do right now. Your father is truly angry because the Council let loose the disciples of Jesus this morning with only a stern warning about preaching in that name. Your grandfather was part of that decision, which has caused your father to look for some reason to remove him from our house. I do not understand what is happening, so be careful.

I showed the note to Stephen. He smiled, then said, "Rejoice, Philip. The Council has released Peter and John."

Then he looked at me. "Does this affect your decision to be baptized?"

"Not in the least," I said. "I fear God more than I fear my father."

18

A New Beginning

"Mother, should we try to make some cow cheese?" asked Tabitha.

"No," answered her mother. "There is little time today, and Shabbat is almost here."

"We've worked on the Sabbath before," answered Tabitha.

"Not this time," she said. "And you'd do well to forget about those times that we broke the law of Moses. You know as well as I do that Jesus died for those sins. Enough now. Talk of something else."

"I wish Jonathan were here. I would like to see him more than the little he has time to visit."

"Well," said Miriam, "if he had his way, you two would not be separated as you are now."

"What do you mean, Mother?"

"You should know, he asked your father to marry you and offered a mohar of 90 pieces of silver."

"Really! Did Jonathan really ask Father to marry me?"

"Yes, but your father is not in favor of allowing you to marry him."

"Why? Why not?" asked Tabitha.

"For that, you must ask your father."

Tabitha was finishing her work as she tried thinking of any reason her father would not approve of Jonathan. She could not understand. She decided to ask him, so she went outside to find him.

"Father, can I talk with you? It's important."

He was tending to one of the sheep. He put his staff away and looked at her.

"What is so important that it cannot wait until evening?"

"Mother told me that Jonathan asked to marry me. Is this true?"

"Yes" was all he responded.

"She also told me that you do not approve of him. Why?"

"It seems that your mother has a lot to say about what I told her not to talk about," he answered. "I did not want you to know about Jonathan's request because I don't believe you should marry him."

"Why? You know that I love him and that he loves me. You know that he can care for me and the family we will make together. I don't understand why you don't want me to marry him after all he has done for this family."

"What has he done for this family?"

"Father, you know well enough. He did not have you arrested when you attacked him and tried to kill him. He kept his father from being at your trial and went searching for you when he found out that you had been beaten and sent home. If he had not found you and brought you home, you would have died on the road. Then when your animals were stripped from you, he replaced them with his own money. Aren't these the actions of an honorable man?"

"What do you mean, he replaced our animals? How do you know this?"

"Stephen told me that Jonathan gave him the money to replace the animals."

"Tabitha, you don't understand. His father is an extremely powerful man, and he doesn't like that I told his son how he used his power to take my brother's farm away from him. His father will not accept you into his house. You will be unwelcomed there. I don't want that for you. I want you to have a happy marriage. Jonathan is an honorable man, but he is a part of the wrong family. I hope that you understand. My mind is made up on this matter."

"But Father—" she started to say.

"Tabitha. It's complicated. If Jonathan finds out that we have been baptized in the name of Jesus, he may turn us in. I want to continue to help with the new converts and help provide food for them. If Jonathan finds out what we are doing and tells his father, that will be the end. We may even be jailed. I want no more talk of this. Do you understand."

"But Father . . ."

"I said no more talk of this. That is final."

"Yes, Father," was all she could say. She ran back into the house and began to cry.

After being baptized, I noticed a large crowd of people coming to be baptized too. They were praising God for the healings that the disciples were doing in the name of Jesus of Nazareth. Stephen told me that even Peter's shadow caused healing of people who had faith to believe. He explained that the people who believed in Jesus as the Messiah were all together and shared all things. Several people, including a man named Barnabas of Antioch, sold land and brought it to the disciples so that no one would lack. He also told me that many believers who lived in Jerusalem continued to bring food to help those in need.

"The day is almost gone, and the Sabbath approaches," I told Stephen. "I will see you later."

"Jonathan, Jesus said that the Sabbath was made for man; man was not made for the Sabbath."

On the way home, I looked at Mathias and wondered if he would share my baptism with my father.

"Do you believe in Jesus as I do?" I asked him.

"I don't have the faith that you have, Master, but I hope to have it soon. I would like to feel the peace that I now see in your eyes." He stopped and looked at me. "Your secret is safe. I will not tell your father what we have done today."

"Thank you," I said. I realized that I could not ask for a better friend. We arrived at home just as it was getting dark. The shofar sounded the beginning of Shabbat.

⫷⬥⫸

The first day of the week was going to be a busy day for me. I called Mathias to my room.

"Sit down, Mathias. I have a gift for you. One, I think, will make you happy." Mathias sat down but protested about receiving any gifts. I handed him a small scroll. It was written in Greek, Latin, and Hebrew and gave Mathias his freedom. Slowly he read the scroll. Then he read it again and looked at me.

"You are free," I said. "You can go, or you can stay. I don't know if I can live without you, and I don't want to try, but you are not mine. You are not a possession; you are a man, a very honorable man. A better friend than any I could find."

"I never thought this day would come," he said, holding the scroll. "The life I knew before I came here is gone. I have no home to return to. This is my home. You are my master. I took an oath to protect and serve you. That oath must be ful-filled."

"Then fulfill it as a friend but not as a slave," I said.

———◆———

The walk to Bethlehem took us a little over an hour. At the city gates, I found several elders and showed them the scroll from Grandfather. They remembered it being purchased many years ago by Gamaliel bar Yaakov for his first grandson.

"He is my grandfather," I said. "He has given me the land. I would like to sell it. Would you help me negotiate a sale to the sheep farmers who currently use it?" They agreed, and by mid-day, the sale was completed, recorded, and the money was collected. Mathias and I returned to Jerusalem.

Some of Jesus' disciples were baptizing at the Pool of Siloam. Stephen was among them. He seemed glad to see me.

"I need to talk to John," I told him.

"Is there a problem?"

"No. I've just sold a piece of land in Bethlehem, and I wanted to contribute to the work that you are doing here."

"Follow me," he said. "I don't know if John is back yet, but I will take you to him."

When we got there, I noticed many people.

"Are these all followers of Jesus?" I asked Stephen.

"Yes. Most of the people who were baptized on Pentecost have returned to their homes in various countries, but many are still here. We feed them, teach them, and see to their needs," answered Stephen.

"How?" I asked.

"Everyone has a job to do that contributes to the whole group. Believers who still live in Jerusalem bring food and stay for the teachings. People like Ruben and Miriam bring cheese and bread. Others bring oil and wine. Some bring vegetables or olives and grapes."

I asked Stephen about John again.

"Peter and John were arrested yesterday for teaching in the temple about Jesus," Stephen said. "During the night, an angel released them and told them to continue their teaching, so they went back to the temple this morning. They may not be back yet."

"You believe that they are coming back?" I asked him. Stephen's faith was beyond belief. The rulers of Israel were set on stamping out the name of Jesus of Nazareth. If they didn't have them stoned to death, they would put them in prison and never let them out.

John appeared in a doorway. He was with another man, and his eyes smiled when he saw me. They came over to me, and John said, "Jonathan, I want you to meet Peter. I have told him about you. Stephen and Philip tell me that you have accepted Jesus as your Messiah. I knew, in time, that you would join us."

"I came to help." I took the bag with the money I received from the land sale and handed it to them. "I'm sure that you can use this better than I can."

Peter looked at me, smiled, and said, "Jonathan, the Master has a purpose for you. You will discover that purpose soon. Remember, you are a new person now. Old things have passed away. All things are new."

"What does that mean?" I asked.

Peter said, "When you were baptized, you died with

Christ. Don't cling to the past, Jonathan. Jesus will use you wherever you go to increase the faith of others."

"If you would like to help, you could assist Stephen, Philip, and Timon as they baptize the new believers at the Pool of Siloam," said John.

"Of course," I said. "I would be happy to help."

19

ARE YOU ONE OF HIS DISCIPLES?

Father was waiting for me when I got home. He knocked on my door and entered my room before I could say anything. I could tell that he was agitated and in a foul mood.

"Jonathan, I need an explanation!"

"About what?" I asked.

"Your grandfather. What has he told you?"

"Grandfather has been a great teacher, but I'm not exactly sure what you are talking about."

"I want to know what he told you about his relationship with this Jesus. What did he tell you?"

"Why don't you ask him," I answered.

"I sent him home. After what he did, I didn't want him around influencing my family."

"I can't believe that Grandfather would do anything to intentionally hurt this family. What exactly did he do?"

"He turned the Council against the wishes of the High Priest. He caused the Council to release those disciples of Jesus by telling them to be careful, or we might find ourselves fighting against God himself. We could have put an end to this Jesus rebellion, but he intervened and let them go. So, I told him to go."

"He is your father. What kind of respect does that show him?" I asked.

"A father has to earn respect, and he has never earned mine. He has never approved of me or the way I get things done. I have no respect for him," he said. "Now, what did he tell you? Is he one of the followers of that rebel?"

"Grandfather told me many things. One of the things he told me was that you knew who you were crucifying. Is that true, Father? Did you know or even suspect that Jesus was the Messiah? That you condemned him anyway, all for political gain?" I asked. The volume of my voice was a little louder than I wanted it to be. I knew that if my father got upset, I would get no answers.

"I told you that your grandfather did not approve of me or what I do. I do not think that Jesus was anything more than another one of those who have come before him pretending to be something that he is not. When the Messiah comes, we will know. Everyone will know. The Romans are still here. Your precious Messiah, as you call him, did not rid us of these gentiles who steal our money, rape our women, and dishonor our God. If your Jesus was the Messiah, he would have driven away this curse that is upon us. But he didn't. I'm telling you, Jonathan, he was not what he pretended to be. Now, are you going to answer my question or not?"

"That's a question he must answer for himself," I replied.

"Then," my father said, "let me ask that question about you. Are you one of the disciples of Jesus?"

I remembered what Stephen told me that Jesus said, "If you deny me before men, I will deny you before my father who is in heaven."

"Father, our nation started with Abraham who was promised that his descendants would be a blessing to the whole world by—"

"I don't need a history lesson, Jonathan," his father interrupted him. "All I need is an answer to my question! Are you or are you not a disciple of Jesus of Nazareth?"

"If you want my answer, then you will listen to the whole truth. If not, this conversation is over." I turned to walk out of my room when he stopped me.

"I will listen," he said. "but don't expect me to become one of his disciples."

With all the love and respect I could muster, I explained to my father what he already knew. I showed him how the life of Jesus fulfilled all the prophecies starting with Moses and going thru Malachi. I reminded him of the prophecy of Daniel that named the time the Anointed One would appear, the writings of Isaiah that described the manner of the death of the Anointed One, and Zechariah's picture of the Anointed One as a lowly and humble king. I showed him how the writings in the Tanakh predicted his death and resurrection.

"So, you see, Father, the Council crucified the Messiah as prophesied, and I think that you know it," I finally said. I looked at him, but I could not tell what he was thinking. There was no sense of sorrow or recognition of the truth. He just stared at me.

He finally said, "If what you say is true, the Council did only that which we were directed to do by scripture. We have no guilt."

"That would be true, Father," I replied. "If you had not called down the curse on all Israel by your statement saying, 'His blood be on us and on our children."

He looked at me and said, "Are you one of his disciples?"

"With all my heart," I answered.

"And you believe he was raised from the dead?"

"Yes. Jesus appeared to me in Galilee, by the sea," I answered.

"Jonathan, you've lost your senses. You've gotten caught up in this Messiah hysteria. You have no idea what you are doing. I should have you locked up until you recognize your error and return to worship the God of Israel."

"As you wish, Father. But I still worship Yahweh. Jesus does not replace the law of Moses; he fulfills it."

"That's blasphemy, Jonathan! Don't you ever say that in my hearing again." He left my room.

A few days later, Mathias woke me with bread and olive oil, a few eggs, and some cheese.

"The cheese is from Tabitha," he said. "She said that she thinks of you often." He had a grin on his face.

"Why are you smiling?" I asked.

He said nothing but continued to smile.

"I'm going this morning to help with the believer's baptism at the Pool of Siloam. I told Stephen that I would be there today," I said. "Do you want to come with me?"

"Yes," he said.

"Are you ready to be baptized?"

"I'm not sure that I understand," he answered.

I tried to explain, "You understand that we are sinners. I know you do. I've explained our belief in the one true God, who is righteous and requires us to be righteous. To please God, we try to follow His law, but we fail. We are all sinners deserving of punishment. Through the Jews, God set up a system of animal sacrifices to cover our sin, but it was not a perfect sacrifice. This is why Jesus came to be crucified. He was God's Son and lived a perfect life. When he died on the cross, he took our punishment so that we could have a relationship with God the Father. Once you believe in your heart that Jesus took our punishment and you desire to trust him with your life, you should be baptized. Do you understand now?"

"Yes and I do believe in him. So, I will be baptized today."

After I finished my small meal, I dressed in common clothes since I didn't want to bring attention to my status as a Levite. We soon left to go meet the others.

When we arrived, I saw Stephen in a debate with the men from the Synagogue of the Freedmen. There were about eight or ten men taking part in the discussion, and it appeared that they were getting angry with Stephen. We were on our way to join the conversation, but the men suddenly left. They were headed for the temple. Stephen joined us as we returned to the Pool of Siloam.

"It appeared that you were having a heated argument with those men," I said.

"Yes," answered Stephen. "Those men are from Alexandria, Cilicia, and Asia. I was hoping to convert them to the Way. When they went home, they could spread the gospel, but they refused to believe the scriptures."

"What is the Way?" I asked Stephen.

"That's the name given to the followers of Jesus. Jesus said that we would be hated just like he was hated, because people walked in the darkness rather than the light. He said that a servant is not above his master. If they persecute him, they will persecute us."

We stood talking about the things that Jesus taught—

how he commanded us to love our neighbors, forgive the trespass of others, and share his words. I noticed the group of men who were arguing with Stephen coming to where we were. There were several temple guards with them. When they arrived, one of the temple guards asked, "Which of you is Stephen?"

"That's him," shouted one of the men as he pointed at Stephen.

"You must come with us."

"Why?" I asked. "He's done nothing wrong." The guards grabbed him and led him to the temple. We decided to follow. A crowd was gathering, and they were talking about Stephen saying blasphemous things against the temple and Moses. I knew that these accusations were false. We went up the southern steps to the open court. The guards brought Stephen and his accusers into the council chambers. I was able to squeeze in, but Mathias remained behind.

I could hear the men accuse Stephen of saying that Jesus was going to tear down the temple and do away with the Law of Moses. The high priest asked Stephen if the accusations were true.

When Stephen began to speak, the council chambers became quiet, and his voice resonated throughout the entire temple. His defense was beautiful. He established Moses as the founder of our Jewish nation and the temple as God's house. Then he attacked the elders of the Council as being stiff-necked and uncircumcised in heart. He accused them of killing the prophets and of being murderers of Jesus.

I thought that the Council was going to attack him, but he looked up into heaven and said that he saw Jesus standing on the right hand of God. Everyone covered their ears and began to scream, "Blasphemy!" Men grabbed Stephen and began to drag him out of the council chambers. They dragged him out the eastern gate and threw him into the Kidron Valley. Then they began to stone him. I started to run to his aid but was stopped by Mathias.

"Let me go," I said as I struggled against his grip. "I have to save him."

"You cannot save him, Master."

"But he's my friend."

"Then let him die with honor," he whispered.

I heard Stephen say, "Lord, lay not this sin to their charge," and then he died.

I stood there. I could not get over what I had just seen. He was so willing to die for the gospel, to genuinely love others enough to show them by his death that Jesus was the way. I noticed a young man that I knew returning the coats to Stephen's accusers. Saul was his name. As he walked away, I heard him say that all of Jesus' followers should suffer the same fate. I didn't understand the hate, but I knew what was coming. We left and headed home.

20

My New Home

Father arrived at home later that day. Mother asked him, "Is it true? Did they really stone Stephen?"

"Yes," he said. "There was nothing I could do. The words he spoke were blasphemous. The crowd took over."

"He was like one of our family. Did you even try to stop it?"

"Where's Jonathan?"

He came to my room and knocked softly, waited, then knocked again, a little harder. I knew it was him, but I didn't want to talk to him. He knocked again.

"Enter," I said.

Father entered the room and stood by my desk. I was looking at the floor.

"Jonathan, there was nothing that I could do for Stephen. You know that, don't you?"

"I know that Stephen is dead," I said. "I know that the Council approved of his stoning, and I know that the Council will release its attack dog, Saul, on the rest of us. What I don't know is why? Why are you so afraid of us? Why does the Council hate us? What have we done that will justify what you are planning to do to the followers of Jesus?"

"Jonathan, you must show more respect for the Council," he replied. "There is a great responsibility over the Council.

We must assure the continuance of our nation. It was in the best interest of all Jews that Jesus die. If the people would have erupted in revolt and tried to make him king, the Romans would have crushed us. I know you understand this."

"What about Theudas?" I said as I stood up. "Remember him? Several years ago, he claimed to be the Messiah with about four hundred followers. After he was killed, the Council left his followers alone. Then there was Judas of Galilee. He had many followers, but the Council again left his followers alone. Why do you hate the followers of Jesus? Tell me, Father. Tell me why the Council hates us."

"Jonathan, come to your senses. Don't put yourself in that group. You need to rethink your beliefs about this supposed Messiah."

"I don't think; I know. Jesus was the Messiah for Israel, for me, and for the entire world. If you're going to arrest his disciples, start with me."

"Jonathan, you don't mean that. Think about what you are saying," he said.

I turned and walked out of my room. Mother was standing by the door. She looked at me with pride in her eyes and smiled. She grabbed my hand, pulled me toward her, then kissed me on the cheek. "Go with God, Jonathan," she whispered.

I left the house. Mathias was waiting for me in the court-yard, and we headed for John and Peter. I had to let them know what was coming.

⋙━◆━⋘

Miriam and Tabitha arrived home with their cheese wagon. They cleaned the cheese out of the wagon and went inside. Miriam called for Ruben to come into the house.

"The Council had Stephen stoned today," she told him.

"Why would they stone Stephen?"

"The way I heard it was that he was preaching about Jesus, and they had him stoned. They said that he spoke blasphemies, and the crowd dragged him outside the temple and stoned him. Ruben, I'm frightened. Do you think they know that we have been baptized?"

"After what I've been through with the High Priest and with Jonathan's father, I don't think they will question that we are followers of Jesus."

"Ruben, what should we do?" asked Miriam.

"I will speak with Peter in the morning. He will know what to do."

"But tomorrow is the Sabbath. Do you think it's wise to go to see Peter?"

"Don't worry. I can go to Peter's home and return. It's within the allowed distance for Shabbat."

"Why don't we pray for guidance," suggested Tabitha.

⁓◆⁓

"Do not be troubled, Jonathan," said Peter. "Stephen is with Jesus. Jesus said that he was going to prepare a place for us, and that he would come and receive us to himself."

"I am saddened by the loss of Stephen. He was a good friend, but I am concerned about what the Council will do to the followers of Jesus now," I explained.

"Jesus will be with us in this time of persecution," John said. "It is a great joy for us to be considered worthy to suffer for Christ, but I understand your concern. Perhaps we should advise those who have come from other lands to return home and share the good news of Jesus."

It was getting dark, so we stayed with the disciples for the sabbath. We shared the Lord's Supper and listened to the teachings about Jesus most of the night. The next day I was surprised to see Ruben talking with Peter. Peter called me over.

"Ruben has heard about the stoning of Stephen, and he is concerned. Do you think that your father will cause trouble for Ruben and his family?" Peter asked.

"Yes," I answered. "There are now two people he wants to make examples of, you, because you revealed his greed to me, and me, because I love Jesus. I think that he will come for me first. He believes that if he jails me, I will stop believing that Jesus is our Messiah."

"You believe that Jesus is the Messiah?" Ruben asked.

"Jonathan was baptized and received the Holy Spirit just like you, Ruben. He has contributed a sizable sum of money to our work here, and he came yesterday to warn us of the coming persecution."

"This means that you are no longer a part of your family," Ruben said. "This is okay with you?"

"I am an adopted son and heir in the family of Jesus the Christ. That is all I want. That is all I need."

"What should I do?" asked Ruben.

"I would prepare to leave the city."

"Where should I go?"

"Sabaste," I replied.

"Sabaste! That city is in the middle of Samaria. I don't want to go to Samaria," he responded.

"You and your family will be safe there. Go and spread the news about Jesus," I answered him.

※

On the first day of the week, Mathias and I went to the Pool of Siloam to baptize the new disciples.

"Are you Jonathan bar Joshua, grandson to Gamaliel bar Yaakov?" I looked up.

"I remember you," said Saul. "We studied together with your grandfather."

"Yes," I replied. "I remember. As you see, I now have the use of my legs. I was healed by Jesus of Nazareth."

"I have papers from the Council to arrest you" was his next sentence. He had several Roman soldiers with him, so I knew I was headed for the Antonia Fortress.

"I'm sure that you have. They are probably signed by my father. Before you take me, may I give final instructions to my servant?" He nodded, and I walked over to Mathias and said in a low voice.

"Take this purse and give it to Ruben. Tell him to go to Sabaste in Samaria and wait for me. When I am free, I will find him."

"Are you sure that you will be freed?" he asked. "There are only two guards. I can take them easily, Master, and then we can get away."

"No. Please do what I ask. Get Ruben and his family to safety in Sabaste."

"As you wish, Master."

I turned and walked to where Saul was. One of the soldiers tied my hands behind my back. We left for the fortress, or so I thought. Instead of going into the fortress, we went to the temple. I was taken into one of the anti-chambers where my father, Caiaphas, and at least twenty members of the High Council were waiting for me.

"Jonathan, I regret to have to bring you to this meeting

under these circumstances. Your father tells us that you have indicated that you believe that this Jesus is the long-awaited Messiah. Although I know your father to be an honorable man, I really wanted to hear from you what your thoughts were on this matter. Would you like to enlighten me on your beliefs?" Caiaphas asked.

"I will be more than happy to answer any question you might have," I said. "Ask me what you want to know, but first tell me if this is a trial and if I am accused of anything," I answered.

"No, this is not a trial and as of yet, you are not accused of anything," he answered. "We just needed some information from you."

"Then, why are my hands tied? And why am I being treated as a common criminal or someone who has broken the law?"

"If you will answer a few questions, this matter can be cleared up, and you can be on your way," said my father.

"Is this how you interrogated Jesus when you tried him illegally," I asked my father. "It did you no good, he still rose from the dead."

Suddenly, arguments broke out between the Pharisees and the Sadducees over the resurrection of the dead. The arguments were getting louder and louder. Caiaphas was unable to control the Council, so he called Saul over and instructed him to bring me to jail. I smiled at Saul.

"I wouldn't smile knowing where you're going," he said.

I was taken inside the Antonia Fortress where we waited until finally, the quartermaster came to his desk. Saul gave him the papers from the Council and I was taken to a cell. Inside the cell, I was shackled to long chains attached to the wall. There were no windows, and the stench took my breath away. I could hear men screaming and the clanging of iron. I knew it would be a sleepless night.

By the third night, I leaned against the wall and fell asleep. I had gotten used to the smell and the noise. In the middle of the night, the room filled with light. It was difficult to open my eyes, but I heard a voice. It was a voice I had heard before.

"Jonathan, go to the Isle of Cyprus. I have work for you there." Then the light vanished.

I asked, "I'm in chains; how can I go to the Isle of Cyprus?" But the cell stayed silent. I tried to go back to sleep, but sleep did not come.

The next morning, the door to the cell was opened. A Roman soldier unlocked the shackles, and I could see where the skin was missing, and the blood had dried. I stood as Amir Ben Remiel entered the cell.

"I have secured your release from the Romans. You need not worry about the High Council of Jewish elders. They will not bother you again. Now, your father is another matter. He would not listen to reason. He wants you to come into agreement with his ambitions, which I know you will not do," he said as he pointed to the door.

As we left, I thanked him for the intervention and asked how my sister, Abigail, was doing. He said that he and his son were extremely pleased with her and offered me a place at his home in Magdala for as long as I needed it. I thanked him but declined. I headed for home. When I arrived, I found that my room had been searched by Father. Mother saw me and came into my room.

"Your father has taken the documents given to you by

Tribune Marcus. He wants you to stay in Jerusalem under his authority," she said.

"He took copies," I said. "The originals are with the shulchani under my seal. He cannot get to those."

"You don't know your father, Jonathan."

"I know that I'm going to the Isle of Cyprus. Jesus told me he has work for me to do there."

"Jonathan," she sighed.

"I love you, Mother. I always will. Tell Father that I love him also. I know he won't believe it, but in time he will understand," I said as I was gathering clothing and packing my scrolls.

"When will you return?" she asked.

"That is in God's hands," I said, "but you are welcome in my house anytime you want to come."

"You have no house," Father said. I didn't know how long he had been there, but he was visibly upset.

"Father, my ownership of these properties are written in Roman law. The writings in our Jewish law will not be powerful enough to grant you your wish of taking from me what the Tribune has given me. It has all been filed and registered in the ledgers of Rome. You cannot change it."

"If you persist in following Jesus, you are no longer my son. You are cut off. Leave my house and never return," he said, then stormed out of the room.

I finished gathering my belongings, embraced my mother, and set out on my journey.

The ride to Sabaste seemed to go on forever. I had taken three horses that were mine and all of my possessions. When

I arrived in the city, I asked if anyone knew where Mathias was staying. Everyone knew where the big Greek was staying, and it did not take me long before I found him. He was with Ruben and his family. When Tabitha saw me, she ran to embrace me.

"I thought that you were dead by now," she said. "I'm so glad to see you again!" Then she stepped away from me and looked at her father. I resisted the urge to take her into my arms again.

"I want you to know, Ruben, that I've been officially removed from my father's family. Therefore, I must start one of my own."

Mathias and I took care of the horses and unpacked our belongings. The home they were staying in had no stable, so I instructed Mathias to take them to a local stable and board them, then I went inside.

"What are you going to do now?" Ruben asked.

"I have a villa on the Isle of Cyprus," I answered him. "Jesus is sending me there. He said that he had work for me there. You are welcome to come. It is in a Jewish settlement, and I'm sure they need cheese."

"What do you mean when you say Jesus has work for you?" he asked.

I explained what happened to me on the first day of the week, about my arrest, my trial before my father and some of the Council, my being put in a cell, and how, on the third night, Jesus gave me my instructions. I told them of how Amir Ben Remiel freed me and what he said about the Jewish Council. Then I told them about my final encounter with my father.

"I would not return to Jerusalem if I were you," I told

him. "Please come with me to Nocisia. It is in a large Jewish settlement, and I know you can find work."

He looked at his wife and daughter, then nodded. Mathias returned and informed me that we must secure rooms to get stable privileges, so he took two rooms for us at the inn.

"Tomorrow we will leave for Caesarea. With the help of Tribune Quintus Magnus, we will be on our way to Cyprus within a few days," I told them.

We arrived at Caesarea on the first day of the week, having spent the Sabbath at Narbata. We found the same inn that we stayed in previously and made arrangements for our animals. Mathias and I set out to find Tribune Quintus Magnus. He knew we were there and sent a few soldiers to escort us to his home. He seemed glad to see us but not surprised. We found out that he had been recalled to Rome. The emperor needed him to take his place in the senate to help consolidate the emperor's power. Julius Cassius would have a ship ready for us in three days. The Tribune was coming with us to Cyprus for a few days, and then he would travel on to Rome.

The day of our departure from Israel came quickly. Being with Tabitha was wonderful, and I renewed my hope that her father would allow us to marry. As the boat set sail, we turned to look at the shoreline as it slowly disappeared. She took my hand, looked up at me, and smiled. I was home.

EPILOGUE

The villa was enormous and beautiful. The stone buildings had large marble columns and beautiful mosaics on the floors. The upper floors of the villa looked out over the Mediterranean Sea.

Jonathan and Tabitha were married in a traditional Jewish ceremony. Miriam and Ruben continued to make cheese, which was sold in the Jewish community. In addition, Miriam helped take care of Jonathan and Tabitha's children. Mathias remained with Jonathan, and eventually he took a Greek wife from the village.

As things settled down, Jonathan began to see what work Jesus had for him. He and Ruben began to share the gospel with the people in their community. God gave Jonathan wisdom in debates and discussions to the point that even the rabbi accepted Jesus as the Messiah. They held regular baptisms in the pool at the villa, which became the meeting place for the new "Christians," as they were now called.

Years would pass before Jonathan and Saul (now named Paul) would meet again. It was in Salamis where Paul first came to Cyprus. Paul, Barnabas, and Mark stayed at the villa for several days, teaching and helping the new church. Jonathan went with Paul as he spread the gospel throughout the island. When Paul left from Paphos, he gave instructions to Jonathan to look after the believers on the island, and this Jonathan did with all of his heart.

About the Author

Robert Picou was born in a small town in southern Louisiana. After high school and military service, he completed his degree in history education and began teaching. He has always had a passion for history, especially ancient history. He has spent over thirty years ministering to young adults. Now he is retired with the desire to write historical fiction novels about the gospel of Jesus Christ. He lives with his wife in Louisiana and can be reached at rapicou@gmail.com.